i

MAR 2 3 2010

PL

THE CROSSING

Gary McMillan

**Cover Concept and design by
Michael McMillan**

**Authors' Discovery Cooperation, Inc.
11308 West Kassnar Dr.
Odessa, Texas 79764**

THE CROSSING

ISBN -978-0-9794443-3-3

DEDICATION

I dedicate this book to the memory of my father who passed away in 1985, and to my mother who still resides in my hometown of Levelland, Texas. My love of 'The Old West' can be traced to them. When I was growing up, only two types of books could be found in our home; the Bible and western novels. 'Thanks' to you both.

PREFACE

Ben Watkins had been a well known mountain man during the years when beaver pelts were in great demand in the East. After the days of the mountain man, he settled along the Border of Texas and Mexico with his wife. Tye, their son was born in 1839, and named after Ben's grandpa.

At a very early age, Ben began teaching Tye everything he needed to know to survive; reading sign, tracking, fighting, and shooting. Tye honed these lessons over the years. Later he became Chief of Scouts at Fort Clark, Texas. He was becoming a legend along the Border; feared by both the bandits and the Apache.

Tye was on his way back to Fort Clark from San Antonio where he had spent his honeymoon when he learned of more Apache trouble. A young buck, Grey Owl, was leading several young Apaches and raising bloody hell along the Border.

Far to the north, an old mountain man was headed south toward Fort Clark. Shakespeare McDovitt had been Tye's father's best friend back in the twenties and early thirties while trapping in the Rockies. He know Ben was dead and now, at seventy-one years old, Shakespear was determined to see his friend's son before it was too late. He didn't know just how much trouble he was headed into.

ABOUT THE AUTHOR

Gary was born and raised in Texas. He loves reading stories of the men and women who risk all to settle the 'Old West'. As a boy growing up, his parents only allowed three types of reading material in their home, the Bible, western books and western magazines.

Gary found the history of Fort Clark very interesting. He has spent the last twenty-five years visiting Fort Clark and researching the history of this particular Fort. 'The Crossing' is the second book in a series about the problems along the Texas-Mexico Border shortly after the Civil war.

THE CROSSING

Chapter I

Late evening shadows were slowly creeping across the rocky ground toward the porch of the adobe house. The old man opened the door and stepped out on the porch, took a quick look around, then sat down on the top step. Bill Farley was 58 years old and had been living here just short of five years with his wife, Clara. Their life together, as most pioneer families, had been one of many hardships, but their love had with stood all of them for thirty-one years. Now, despite the recent tragedy of their son being killed, life seemed to be getting easier. Bill had just finished a good evening meal, and he was content to do what he always did at this time of day; sit on the porch, smoke his pipe, and watch the always spectacular Texas sunset. He had a powerful lot of thinking to do and he always seemed to do it best at this time of day.

Bill and Clara's only son, Robert, had been killed along with his wife, a month earlier in a raid by a band of Comanche about 150 miles to the north. They had hidden their eight year old son, Jason, in a cellar and he escaped death, but had watched the horrible murder of his parents. He had been living with Bill and Clara for a week now, and he seemed to be slowly adjusting to his new surroundings. Bill thought the youngster was getting over the trauma of his parents death, if one could ever completely forget something like that. Bill knew the boy filled a void that had been in his and Clara's life since there had been no children around after Robert had left home. That had been almost ten years ago.

Bill filled his pipe and as he lit it, Jason came out with the rifle and handed it to his grandpa. Bill checked to make sure it was loaded, then propped it against one of the post supporting the roof over the porch. It had been awhile since any Apaches had bothered him, but to survive out here a man had better not let his guard down for a second. Jason sat down on the top step beside his grandpa.

"Get enough to eat, boy?"

"Yes sir, Grandpa. My old belly's bout ready to plumb bust," Jason said, rubbing his stomach.

"Only reason I married your grandma, Jason, was she could always cook." Jason had a bewildered look on his face at the statement. Bill reached over and with his big calloused hand, tousled Jason's hair while laughing.

"Just joshing boy. I love everything about your grandma; always have." He looked up at the hills.

"Look at that sunset, Jason. There's nothing like a Texas sunset. Nothing in the world could be prettier." Jason looked at the sun dropping behind the hills and marveled at the many different colors that he could see thru the scattered clouds: orange, yellow, black and all the colors in between against a backdrop of light blue. It was pretty he thought, real pretty.

Bill put his arm around Jason and both sat there looking. Jason was the only remaining male that would carry on the Farley name and Bill was going to keep him close, and safe. Neither was aware of what was on top of the hill watching them.

~~~

Grey Owl, stretched out on the ground behind two large cedars, studied the homestead which stood fifty yards below him. He knew from two previous days of watching that the man and the boy would come out on the porch before the sun set behind the hills. The older man would light a pipe and both would sit on the steps of the porch. He would be able hear their voices but did not understand the words being said, but he did not need to; he knew the man would be looking at the sunset and telling stories to his son just as Grey Owl's father had told him so many times in the past. Those were the good times and he longed for them. It seemed a long time ago but actually had only been five or six winters ago. It was before the white man had descended on this land like a great flood, changing everything for the Apache.

He glanced behind him where the men who were with him waited his signal to attack. He looked back to the white man's house just as the old man came out and, as previous nights, sat down on the porch. The younger one came out and handed the rifle to the old man. Each of the men with Grey Owl was like he was, young and untested in battle. Each was anxious to prove his manhood the only way an Apache knew; in battle. Grey Owl knew they were anxious, but he was waiting on the sun to be directly behind him as it dipped below the hills. He saw the white man had a rifle by his side, but he also knew it was hard to be accurate with the sun in your eyes, no matter how good a shot you were.

Grey Owl had a rifle but only two of the men with him had one, the rest had bows. He and the two with rifles only had seven bullets between them, but this problem would be solved soon. He knew the white men always had plenty of weapons and ammunition in their homes. He intended for all his men to have a rifle and bullets within the next few days from the white invaders he planned to kill.

He again looked over his shoulder at the setting sun. It would be in the perfect spot to blind the white man in a few short minutes. At this distance, it was no disadvantage for an Apache to use a bow instead of a rifle. He was as accurate with it as he was with a rifle at fifty yards. He signaled his four best bowmen to crawl to him. They quickly lay on each side of him. At his signal, they would stand and release their arrows.

As previously planned, the remaining braves made their way back down the hill and into a small creek bed that ran within forty yards of the white man's corral where four horses were stabled. They would rush the house from that side when the arrows were released from the top of the hill. It would be so easy.

Grey Owl again glanced over his shoulder to check the position of the sun. He looked back down at the homestead and prepared to give the signal. Hesitating for a moment, he shut his eyes and thought about the vision he had last night. In the vision his father's brother, Lone Wolf and the fierce war chief, Tanza, appeared astride their prancing ponies. Fire appeared to be coming from the pony's nostrils and their eyes were as red as burning coals. Both men wore white breechcloths, white knee high moccasins, and a white bandana atop their heads. They were bare chested, and both had a single broad stripe of white paint across their face. Their long raven colored hair was blowing in the wind as lightning flashed, and the thunder roared; from a clear blue sky.

Tanza stopped his horse and looking straight at Grey Owl, raised both hands above his head, and looked up at the sky. The wind stopped, as did the lightning and thunder. It was suddenly very strange. An eerie silence fell across the land. Tanza lowered his arms to his side, and slowly lowered his head until he was looking into Grey Owl's eyes. He began to speak to Grey Owl, and his words were clear, yet his lips were not moving.

"Brother, it is your time. It is your time to rise up and lead your people against these invaders who are taking our land and herding our people like so many cattle to the camps. It is time for our people to quit bowing to these white men and live the Apache life, like our fathers, and their fathers did...free. It is your time, Grey Owl. Lead your people and drive these invaders from our land."

Grey owl had awakened from the vision sweating. He was shocked at how clear he could see and hear the two men he had admired most. He hated the bluecoats and especially the scout Watkins, who had personally killed Lone Wolf and Tanza. He was sure the vision showed the Great Spirit was smiling on him, and he would be the one to lead his people to victory. He opened his eyes, and raised his arm to give the signal to attack.

As the braves in the creek bed approached the stables, one of the horses in the corral began snorting and stomping his feet. The white man was up immediately, and grabbing his rifle looked in the direction of the corral, his back now toward Grey Owl. Grey Owl knew this was his chance with the white man looking away and he signaled the men to stand and release their arrows. The boy, still sitting on the porch, was hit square in the chest with one arrow and another in his thigh. The old man was as tough as nails. He was hit in the side and leg but did not go down.

With loud shrieks, the Apaches came from the creek bed. The man kneeled down and fired his single shot Sharps and one brave was hit while in full stride knocking him backwards, a hole the size of a small fist in his back where the bullet exited. Knowing he would not have time to reload the man turned and stumbled to where the boy lay. Seeing he was obviously dead he headed up the steps into his house. Grey Owl fired his rifle, and saw the bullet hit the man low in the back. The force of the bullet knocked the man across the porch, into the door. The man turned and faced the charging Apaches for a second before he slowly collapsed to a sitting position, his back against the door. A bright red streak covered the door where he slid down. The Apaches were in the yard now, only twenty yards away and coming fast. A blast from one of the windows was followed by another brave stumbling and falling face down in the dirt. The shot did not slow the young warriors and they were on the man quickly. The white man was a fighter. He pulled a Bowie and cut one of the young braves' wrists that were a little slow in reacting to the sudden appearance of the knife. He held the knife in front, cutting edge up, shouting at them in words they did not understand.

Two arrows in his chest ended the old man's struggle. The door opened and a woman stood there, a rifle in her hand, and as she squeezed the trigger it was wrenched from her by a brave standing beside the door. The bullet went harmlessly into the air. She looked at the body of her grandson, at her husband's, then at her empty hands. Suddenly it was as if everything was moving in slow motion. She saw the Apaches and slowly backed up, watching them as they closed in. She knew what was coming, and reached for a knife that was on the table. Grasping the handle, she was plunging the long blade into her chest when her arm was grabbed, and held. Realizing it was useless to struggle; she shut her eyes and prayed that they would kill her quickly. Her clothes were stripped from her as she was thrown to the floor. Grey Owl let some of his braves have their way with the woman and then had her killed and scalped. The boy was scalped also, but not the old man, the Apache's sign of respect for a fighting man. The Farleys were gone, and just as it had happened so many times before out here to other families, the hopes, the dreams, and generations of a family name were all erased in less than a minute.

The raiders found a pistol and three rifles along with several boxes of ammunition. Grey Owl was disappointed that two of his men were dead, but they now had more guns and four horses. He was satisfied as the sun set, and darkness settled in. He made a mistake in not thinking of the horses alerting the man to their presence. It was a mistake that cost two of his friend's lives, but it was a mistake he would never make again. Three bottles of the white man's whiskey was found and the young warriors started drinking in celebration of their victory, despite Grey Owl's strong protest. It was two hours before daylight when the braves, in a drunken stupor, finally set fire to the house.

If he could kill a few more whites, capture more horses; acquire more rifles and bullets, more Apaches would come to him. He knew the bluecoats would be after him quickly and he was looking forward to the battles. He wanted to kill the man who scouted for the bluecoats, this man who had killed his friend Tanza, and his father's brother, Lone Wolf; this man who had caused so much misery for his people. Yes, this man had caused much suffering for the Apache, but at the same time was greatly respected by all Apaches as a fighter and as a great warrior.

"Soon I will kill the great warrior scout Watkins, and the name of Grey Owl will be shouted in all the wickiups of the Apache," he said to no one in particular. Smiling, he led the warriors into the darkness of the night, away from the burning homestead.

~~~

Lieutenant James Rogers opened the curtains of the single window in his small hotel room. The dim light of his kerosene lamp filtered out onto Main Street in San Antonio. Looking out, he could see no one moving about. He did see a man curled in a fetal position on the boardwalk across the street. After watching him for a couple minutes and seeing no movement, he wasn't sure if he was dead or alive. Curious, he continued to watch the man and finally, he was relieved to see him move slightly, and then slowly sit up.

"Well at least he's not dead," he muttered to himself. He laughed a minute later when the man stood up, took two steps, and fell flat on his face on the packed dirt of Main Street.

"Hell, he's just a drunk, suffering for his sins of last night," he said as he pulled the curtain closed. He shook his head and chuckled to himself.

Checking his brand new gold pocket watch, a present from his father for his graduation from the Point, he saw that it was a few minutes before five a.m.

"God won't this night ever get over with?" he mumbled. Rogers had slept very little this night and little the night before. As a matter of fact, he hadn't slept a hell of a lot since he found himself assigned to this barren country. He had been dressed and pacing

9

the floor for over a hour, anxious for the coach that was due this morning to take him to Fort Inge which was about seventy miles west of San Antonio. This was his first assignment since he graduated from the Point, and not knowing what kind of reception he would receive from the other officers and the enlisted men, or exactly what was going to be expected of him, he was as nervous as a virgin bride on her wedding night. He felt he could not ever feel more alone.

He was from an upper middle class family in Washington and had joined the army fully expecting, through his father's connections, to get a cushy assignment in the East. He never expected to be assigned to a frontier outpost and sure as hell not in a place as Godforsaken as this country. He walked over to the dresser against the far wall and looked at himself in the cracked mirror, brushed some lint off his blue tunic, straightened his yellow kerchief, and placed his hat on his head, adjusting the angle to his liking.

"Damn sharp if I say so myself."

He was of medium height, about five nine, and weighed in the neighborhood of one hundred fifty pounds. He sported a mustache below his prominent nose, had deep blue eyes, and hair that was the same color as his mustache, blonde. While visiting with some of the officers that were assigned here in San Antonio, one jokingly commented what a prize that blonde mop would be for some Apache buck. Everyone had laughed at the comment, including Rogers, but the comment stuck with him. For the first time in his life he wished that maybe his hair was brown or black, like most everyone else. He wondered if he really would be singled out and targeted by the Apache. He shuddered at the thought.

He was hoping some of the officers could tell him what to expect but not a single one of them had

10

been any farther west, and none had seen any action. They could only tell him what they had heard from officers they were acquainted with that had been farther west. Some of the stories they told of the Apache made his toes curl. He was told of the many outlaw gangs that roamed the border of Texas and Mexico and the miserable living conditions he would face. None of this had made him feel any better about the situation. He just wished he could speak with someone that had been out there; someone who could fill him in on things he needed to know.

He had graduated close to the top of his class at the Point and he knew the manual frontwards and backwards. He wasn't concerned about his not knowing what to do in any situation. Yes, he knew what to do, but would he be able to do it when the time came. He was a better than average horsemen, and he was an expert with a rifle or pistol, at least on the firing range. How he would handle them when someone was shooting back was a question that lay in the back of his mind and would not go away. In fact, he didn't know whether he would run or fight when the time came... he had never had to.

The sun still had not made its appearance when he left his hotel room and went downstairs to the restaurant. While eating a hearty breakfast of steak and eggs, an officer he had met the day before but could not recall his name, came with his cup of coffee in his hand and sat down at his table.

"You leaving on the coach this morning?" he asked.

Rogers nodded his head. "Supposed to be here about mid morning."

"Still looking for someone to tell you what to expect?"

"Yeah, but looks like that is not a happening

thing."

"Maybe it will. This may be your lucky day, Lieutenant."

"How's that?" Rogers asked, chewing on a biscuit.

"Tye Watkins is going to be on the coach with you. He and his wife are going back to Fort Clark which is about forty or so miles farther west of where you are going at Fort Inge. They've been here on their honeymoon."

"TYE WATKINS...the Scout?" Rogers blurted out, damn near choking on his biscuit. He was suddenly very attentive. "The same one who I have been hearing stories about ever since I arrived here?"

The Lieutenant nodded his head. "You couldn't do better than him to answer any questions you have, if you have any."

"Not more than a thousand or so." Rogers said laughing. He was going to be in a coach with the famous scout for the better part of two days. He raised his coffee cup to his new friend. "You just made my day, Lieutenant." He was definitely looking forward to meeting this man who was becoming larger than life.

~~~

The early morning sun was just starting to add a little light to the hotel room where Tye, propped up on his elbow, lay looking down at the most beautiful woman on earth. He was playing with her long, brown hair that was splayed across her pillow while she slept. As he lay there, his mind drifted back to the events of the past month and a half. He had been instrumental in ridding the country of the most vicious of all the bandit gangs along the Border, the Vasquez brothers. Tanza and his band of Apaches had killed two of his

12

best friends, Jim and Marie Turley, and took the two Turley grandchildren captive. Tye had buried Jim and Marie, and standing by their graves, swore he would get the children back. Three weeks later, after killing Tanza in a vicious knife fight, he made good his promise. He arrived back at Fort Clark to an unexpected hero's welcome by the troops of Fort Clark and the citizens of Brackettville. And last, he had done something he had sworn never to do, he gave up his bachelorhood. He and Rebecca had been married a week ago in the largest shindig that Fort Clark had ever seen.

They had been in San Antonio for a week, enjoying their honeymoon, dining and visiting the sites around the city. The Alamo had an effect on both of them. Tye would have given anything to have met David Crockett. He figured his father, who had been a famous mountain man in his younger days, and Crockett was cut from the same mold. Neither wanted to be around a lot of people, didn't want anyone telling them what to do, always wondering what was on the other side of the hill, and never liked anyone's rights being stepped on.

Tye's exploits had reached the Governor and he and Rebecca had been guests for one evening at the Governor's home. They had lunch one day with the Fifth Military District's Commander, General Reynolds. He had wanted to meet Tye after the reports he had received from Major Thurston, post commander at Fort Clark. He was as impressed with Tye, the man, as he was with the reports and hinted he would like Tye to be available for other trouble areas of Texas.

Today was the last day of their honeymoon as the coach would be leaving about mid-morning to take them back to Clark. Tye was anxious to get back. They'd had a wonderful time, but this type of living would make a man soft in a hurry. This was the first time he had been more than fifty or so miles away from where he was born on the banks of the Rio Grande River. A week in the city convinced him city life wasn't for him. He loved the open spaces and being able to do what he wanted to do, when he wanted to, and not ever having to care about what time it was. While here, he saw firsthand what living in the city was like. People rushing here and rushing there; going to work at a certain time; working all day; trying to get ahead or to keep up with their friends. They had no time to enjoy the little things life had to offer like watching the sun come up, or one of the beautiful Texas sunsets. His thoughts were interrupted by Rebecca's soft voice.

"Morning honey," she said reaching with her hand to place it behind Tye's head pulling him down to her face. He lightly kissed each eye, the end of her pert little nose, and then a long kiss on her lips that had both wanting more. She pulled back and asked.

"What time does the coach leave?"

"In a little while we don't have to hurry," he said snuggling closer.

She suddenly jumped out of bed. "Well it takes me a tad longer to get ready than you." She walked over to the window to look out on the street. Her body was clearly visible beneath the thin night gown and Tye was moving in behind her while she looked out the window and circled his arms around her waist. "We really don't have to hurry," he said. They didn't.

~~~

The coach was on time, and as Lieutenant Rogers was stepping into the coach he saw a tall, very muscular looking man with a beautiful woman on his arm walking toward the coach. "That has to be him,"

14

he thought to himself. He took a seat and was watching the couple approach the coach. The lady was beautiful and any other time he would be watching her, but he was noticing the man more. He moved with a grace that reminded him of a big cat he had seen in a side show one time. You could tell by watching him walk that he was very sure, very confident of himself.

"Howdy Jake." The man he figured to be Watkins hollered at the driver.

"Howdy back to you, Tye," a voice came from atop the coach. "Good to see you and the missus again."

"You going to keep this old coach on the road today?" Tye asked, laughing.

"Just you get in the coach you smart-aleky young smart ass..." He looked at Rebecca and remembered his manners. "Excuse me mam. That sorta slipped out," he said embarrassed.

Rebecca just laughed. "If that's the worse you ever say in front of a lady, I wouldn't worry about it."

Tye took her hand and held it to help her keep her balance while she stepped on the step to climb up into the coach. A hand came out of the coach and took her other hand and helped her inside. She took a seat facing the back of the coach and got a look at the man who had helped her as Tye slid into the seat beside her.

"Thank you, Lieutenant," she said.

Rogers took off his hat and attempted a not very successful bow in the close confines of the coach. "My pleasure, mam."

"Thanks," Tye said and stuck out his hand. "Tye Watkins and this is my wife, Rebecca."

"Ro...Rogers, J...James Ro...Rogers...Lieutenant James Rogers," he finally got

15

the words out.

"My pleasure Lieutenant," Tye said smiling as he sat down beside Rebecca.

With the crack of the whip and a couple of obscenities from Jake, the coach was in motion before Tye got comfortable...at least as comfortable as one could get in these contraptions. They were heading out of San Antonio taking Tye and Rebecca home, and Rogers to he knew not what. Nothing was said for several minutes then Tye spoke up.

"You going to Inge, Lieutenant?"

"Yes sir."

"This your first assignment?"

"Yes sir."

"I'm guessing you just graduated from the Point?"

"Yes sir."

"Can you speak more than two words at a time, Lieutenant?"

"Yes sir." Then he realized Tye was politely mocking his two word answers. "I mean, yes I can." He looked at Tye, then at Rebecca. They were laughing and then he was, too.

"My first assignment, Sir; I'm a little nervous."

Tye looked him over and was thinking, "My God, they are getting younger every day."

"Ever since I heard you were going to be on the coach I have been thinking of things to ask..." he was stopped by Tye holding up his hand.

"Lieutenant, I will answer all your questions the best I can, but right now I want to get some sleep. We've been on our honeymoon you know." He gave Rogers a smile and a wink. Rogers understood and smiled, said he understood just as Tye winced from Rebecca elbowing him in the side for the remark. Rebecca placed her head on Tye's shoulder and was quickly asleep. Tye, staring out the coach's window, was slowly becoming mesmerized by the passing landscape. It was all the same- mesquite, all types of cactus, rocks, cedar, sage, and the short grama grass. It wasn't long before his chin was on his chest and he too was sleeping soundly.

Lieutenant Rogers studied him carefully, thinking of all the stories he had heard about this man. He was big, well over six feet, but if a person believed all the stories about him, one would think he had to be at least eight foot tall. He wondered if he would measure up to this man; he doubted it. From what he had heard, not many could. He looked at the barren, arid land that was outside the coach and wondered, as most men do at first, how he would measure up to the tasks before him. He wondered if he could face an Apache charge without wetting his pants; could he handle a shootout with bandits; could he hold up physically to the demands of this country.

He looked at Tye and shook his head. He heard that he has been doing that since he was fourteen or fifteen. "He would probably laugh if he knew how nervous I was," Rogers thought to himself. He sat and studied the passing country side through the coach's window, wondering why anyone would want to live out here anyway. With that thought, he finally drifted off to sleep.

~~~

Many miles to the northwest, Shakespeare McDovitt was entering the town of El Paso, Texas. It was mid morning and the sun was only half way to its zenith promising today was going to be like yesterday and the day before, hot. Even though it was early, it was not too early for his wanting to quench his thirst with a shot of whiskey. He had been on the trail for almost a month, having come from the southern part of Colorado, slowly making his way toward Fort Clark, Texas, which was still some three hundred or so miles farther south of El Paso.

He was seventy one years old but one would never guess it. He wasn't a big man, five foot seven and one hundred-fifty pounds after he ate a big meal. There wasn't an ounce of body fat on him. His face was tanned and wrinkled from too many years exposure to the sun and the elements, but his deep blue eyes were still as clear as they were when he was twenty. There was still surprising strength and agility in his old frame. Observing his movements from a distance, one would think he was a man of maybe thirty. There was nothing that made him stand out among the other men he saw in El Paso, except his clothes and weapons. He still wore his buckskins and had his knife and tomahawk on his belt. The only difference in his appearance from thirty years earlier when he was trapping beaver in the Rockies and the Yellowstone was that his old flintlock rifle and pistol were gone and had been replaced by a single shot Sharps and a six shot ball and cap Navy pistol.

Shakespeare was one of the original mountain men. He had made a name for himself during those ' Shining Times' in the Rockies and the Yellowstone from about 1815 to 1836. He and his best friend, Ben Watkins, were somewhat over shadowed by their partner, the famous Jim Bridger. Both let it be known over the years that it was only because Jim could tell tales better than they could. Old Bridger loved an audience and he loved to talk.

Shakespeare was making the trek to Fort Clark to see his old friend's son. He had heard Ben had been killed a few years earlier and decided that before he checked it in himself; he wanted to meet his friend's son.   He had heard stories from the troops he scouted for at Fort Bent in southwest Colorado about this scout in Texas that was making quite a name for himself along the Texas/Mexico Border chasing down bandits and Apaches.   This scout was Tye Watkins, his old friend's only son.   He had a letter from Ben that was written years ago and was now well worn from his carrying it around all these years.   It was the only letter he had ever gotten in his whole life.   He couldn't read writing but different people had read it several times to him over the years.   In the letter Ben had invited him to come live with them along the Rio Grande and mentioned he had a son that was going to be something special.   He just never got around to going down there.   Now it was too late to see Ben again but by damn, he was going to see his son.

Entering one of the many saloons on Main Street, he ambled up to the bar and ordered a shot. Downing it quickly, he ordered another and downed it, enjoying the taste and the relaxing affect the whiskey had on his weary old bones.   He, looking in the large mirror behind the bar, surveyed the tables behind him without turning around.   The saloon was almost empty this time of the day but there were three men at one table playing cards.   Picking up his glass of whiskey, he walked over and asked if he could join in.   One of the men looking up and said in a whiskey slurred voice.

"Well, look what we have here...a bonafide old mountain man.   Pull up a chair old timer."   As Shakespeare sat down, the man continued in a sarcastic tone.

"I take it you know how to play this game old timer?"   Shakespeare, though irritated by the man, kept his mouth shut.   He took some twenty dollars out of his pocket and laid the bills and coins on the table in a neat stack.

"Don't look like you aim to play long," the man said laughing while slapping Shakespeare on the back. Shakespeare had enough. "Lookee heer, boy, Yu make wun mo'r reemark aimed at me or yu tech me wun mo' time, I'll interduce yu ta Susie."

The man laughed even louder. "Who the hell is Susie, your squaw?" The next thing he knew, the old man had a vice like grip on his throat and out of nowhere a blade was touching his cheek, just below his right eye.

"This here sunny is Susie," Shakespeare growled. "She's karved up mo'r wun yung pup like yu, tho tha wur Injuns, not white men, but I don't thank she wuld kno tha damn deffrence."

There was a long moment of silence. Sweat was running down the man's face, his eyes wide with fear.

"Now sunny, kan we play without enee mo komments frum yu?" Shakespeare asked in a low voice. The man nodded and Shakespeare released his grip and put Susie back in its sheath. The man took out his kerchief and wiped the sweat off his face.

"Deel tha kards," Shakespeare said. The other two men turned their heads so the loudmouth friend of theirs could not see them smiling. Both knew sooner or later his mouth was going to get him into trouble, maybe dead. Neither said a word when their nervous friend fumbled the cards when shuffling, only a smile crossing their faces.

Chapter II

Tye had become accustomed to the coach's swaying and was sleeping soundly. Years of living on the edge however, had honed his senses to a razor's edge and they were always working, even when he was asleep. The coach was slowing down, approaching a way station, and the slight change in the swaying woke Tye up instantly. Here, there would be a change of horses, giving them enough time to stretch, work the kinks out of their backs and legs and get a bite to eat. The elderly couple that ran the station was friendly and the meal was filling. Jake came in and grabbed a quick bite and then told everyone it was time to get on down the road.

It was mid-afternoon and even with the breeze coming through the open windows, it was hot inside the coach. Not only did the passengers suffer the heat but the dust was a problem also. These things didn't prevent a weary Rebecca from falling quickly asleep again with her head on Tye's shoulder.

"Fire away Lieutenant," Tye said. Rogers looked at him, not quite knowing what he meant.

"Do what?" he asked.

"The questions you said you had," Tye said smiling; "Now's as good a time as any."

"Yes sir," Rogers said. He hesitated for a second, trying to figure out where to start but Tye took the initiative and started talking.

"I figure you are from a family that never lacked

for anything and you probably have never been hungry or suffered any severe hardships in your life." Tye took one of Roger's small hands into his large calloused hand and looked at the palm. "Never had to do much physical labor either; about right so far?"

"I guess you are right. I had it pretty good compared to some of my friends at the Point," Rogers replied.

"I figure you have a lot to learn, Lieutenant." Tye held up his hand when Rogers started to say something. "I'm not questioning your book knowledge so don't get your bowels in an uproar. Why don't you just let me talk and you just listen. If you have a question, just speak up. You will need to realize what I am going to say is not directed at you but just from what I have witnessed in the past: understood?"

"Yes sir," Rogers replied, leaning forward so he could hear better since Tye was keeping his voice down, not wanting to wake Rebecca.

"The first thing young officers like you, that are fresh out of the Point, have to get the chip off their shoulders. By that, I mean the attitude I have seen most of them have is that they think they are a little better than anyone else... they know it all. The people out here won't stand for it, civilians or enlisted men. No matter how smart you are, no matter how much education you have, it doesn't mean a damn thing out here. A man here is measured a little different than where you come from. People measure a man out here by his being a man of his word and doing what he says he will do, not putting himself above anyone else, and never backing down from a fight. Speaking of fighting, it doesn't always matter whether you win or not, just don't back down ever." Tye paused, and stared out the coach's window for a few seconds before continuing.

23

"Listen to those that have been here for awhile, even the enlisted men. And speaking of them, don't expect a real warm welcome from them. They have seen a lot of you "hot shot" Lieutenants that know everything, get some of their friends killed. You will have to earn their respect by making good decisions in the field. When you are in command, you command, but it doesn't hurt to listen to advice from those who have been there, before you make a decision. At first, you will probably be on patrols with other officers   until you learn the lay of the land and get accustomed to the hardships that this land serves up, which is plenty. Learn where the springs are and which one's holds water year around and which don't."

Rebecca raised her head up off Tye's shoulder and looked at the lieutenant.

"You should feel privileged, Lieutenant. I do believe Tye has spoken more words to you in the last five minutes than he has to me in the last week." She looked at Tye and laughed. Tye shrugged his shoulders.

"Just trying to help the Lieutenant, honey." He then looked at Rogers and continued telling him what to expect, hoping maybe to help him in some way to make it without that yellow head of hair hanging on some Apache's spear.

"Don't underestimate the Apache just because he is uneducated. While you were running around in knee pants and playing games, the Apache youngster was learning to track, hunt, read sign, and fight. By the time he is fifteen or sixteen; he has fought his enemies, killed, and took scalps." Rogers started to say something but Tye continued talking.

"The Apache is tough. He will ride his horse till it flounders and then slit its throat, and if he is out of water, he will drink its blood. He can run fifty, sixty

24

miles a day on foot if he has to. He will eat things to survive that would make a white man puke. Another thing, very seldom will you see an Apache unless he wants you to see him. They know they cannot stand toe to toe with the army so they fight a hit and run type of war. Now you see them, now you don't." Tye paused and looked out the window again before continuing.

"Don't underestimate this land either, Lieutenant," he said nodding toward the passing landscape. "It's just like the Apache, merciless and can kill you just as quick as any Apache arrow or a bandit's bullet. The bandits, well that's another story. They are as cruel as the Apache. They have no morals and certainly no qualms about killing another man, red, brown or white. In a way, they are worse than the Apache. You know how you stand with an Apache: well a bandit, he'll shake your hand, pat you on the back, then cut your throat. Neither the bandits nor the Apaches have read any manuals on how to conduct a war or studied the rules of war. They make their own and they are damn good at it." Tye paused for a couple seconds. "Do you have any questions, Lieutenant?"

"You are covering just about everything I was curious about, except," he hesitated a second.

"Except what?" Tye asked.

"Well, I understand what you just said about the Apache but what about his village life, family life? I would like to understand him a little more."

Tye looked at him and suddenly, had a little more feeling for this young man. Not a single new Lieutenant that had asked him for advice had ever asked for his help in understanding the Apache.

"The word Apache comes from a couple of sources; in the Yuma language it means fighting man;

in the Zuni language it means enemy. In any language it means they are a dangerous people. They are vicious in battle but as gentle as a lamb with their children. They are kind and gentle with family but exceptionally cruel to captives. They do not lie and are extremely vengeful if betrayed. Most people call them savages because of the things they do to people, but not me. I respect their way of life, and sorta envy them in a way. I sometimes feel like we are wrong and they are right. They feel this land is theirs. I would be just like them if someone was trying to run me off land I had been on for years and years."

"I understand. I would too," the young Lieutenant said.

"They generally move in small groups, twenty to thirty, and seldom come together with other bands even in times of danger. This has hurt them in their struggle with the Army. If a hundred or so warriors ever got together at one time, it would be a bloodbath not only for the homesteaders, but for the Army as well. This will happen one of these days. The bands move frequently, following the game. They are a proud people and will bow down to no one. The main thing is to remember what I said earlier. When you are on patrol don't relax your guard just because you haven't seen any Apaches. Very few times has the army surprised them. Keep your eyes open and listen to the veterans. That's the best advice I can give you."

"Do you know the post commander or any of the officers at Inge?"

"No, I'm sorry to say I don't. I do know the Chief of Scouts, Ben Wilson. He's a good man and knows his business. You'll do well listening to him."

"I appreciate your telling me all this, Mr. Watkins. I will remember what you said."

"One more thing, Lieutenant, there's times you

will be scared to death. Don't ever let your men see you lose control. A composed officer will hold a bunch of scared troopers that are looking for something, or someone to take control in times of danger. If you lose it, I guarantee you a massacre."

"I know what to do in just about any situation, at least all situations that were in the manual." Rogers said. "I just have never faced anyone trying to kill me. You'll probably laugh but I'm real nervous about that, not knowing how I will react in a situation."

"Every man is a little scared of the unknown," Tye said. "Every man is scared going into a battle."

"That doesn't include you, does it?"

"Sure it does."

"YOU, SCARED," Rogers blurted out. "That's hard to believe."

"If any man tells you he ain't when he is facing another man that's trying to kill him, he's a damn liar, Lieutenant, and he's not a man to trust."

"I just never thought you..." Rogers said but was interrupted again before he could finish.

"What separates one man from another is how he reacts to fear. Some thrive on it, actually enjoy it. Others just do their job and try to stay alive. You have some that can't handle it at all and fall to pieces. I've seen them all. I will say this though, I have yet to ever see one of you Point grads ever get shot in the back," Tye said laughing.

"Is it true that your father was a famous mountain man?"

"He was a mountain man alright. He trapped with Jim Bridger and Shakespeare McDovitt for several years. As far as being famous, well he had some of those cheap dime novels written about him. He always played them down, said the stories were based on fact but a lot was added by the writers. He was

27

educated and he would read the stories to the others that were around the campfire. He said you could hear them hootin', hollering and laughing for a mile.

The sun was dropping behind the low lying hills and had the makings of another beautiful Texas sunset. This had always been Tye's favorite time of the day, whether on the trail or sitting on his porch at his living quarters. There was almost always a few clouds hanging low in the west and the setting sun behind them cast off any number of colors, from pink, to orange, to blood red, to black, depending on how thick the clouds were. A man could do a powerful lot of thinking at that time, sitting back with a smoke, thinking about the day's events, and what's coming tomorrow. This was one of his favorite memories of his early life with his ma and pa. Every evening, they would sit on the porch watching the sunset, listening to the sound the doves and other birds made as they flew in for their evening drink at the stock tank. Best of all, this was when Pa's stories of his adventures with Bridger and McDovitt while trapping the Yellowstone and the Rockies were told. Since those long ago days, his life had been saved more than once when faced with situations with the Apaches by remembering the stories of how Ben handled similar situations with the Blackfoot all those years ago.

Rogers started to say something but old Jake cut loose with some of his colorful language as the coach was slowing for the next station. Here, a new driver would take over and fresh horses would be harnessed. The coach came to a halt and Jake opened the door.

"You going to ride the rest of the way inside with us, Jake?" Tye asked.

"Naw," he hollered back. "I'll ride on top where there is a breeze. I smell like a goat and sure wouldn't want to offend that purty wife of yours." He walked off laughing and then over his shoulder, hollered. "You folks hurry up now. Stretch your legs and get something to eat. We have one more stop before we get to Inge, but it's just a change of horses. There won't be no more food till breakfast at Inge."

It was full dark when they climbed back into the coach. A coyote cut loose with its lonely wailing just as the coach started to move, which Rogers thought was appropriate for the moment. He felt pretty alone too. His new post was only a few hours away and he hoped he could remember half of what Tye had told him. "Thank you Lord for having him on this coach with me," he thought to himself.

When arriving at the next station, they got out of the coach only long enough to relieve themselves and walk a short distance to get the kinks out. Within ten minutes they were on the last leg to Inge. It didn't take long for the three to be sleeping soundly.

~~~

Shakespeare had played cards for most of the day. He had some luck and was walking away about forty dollars richer than when he sat down. The loudmouth man had kept his mouth shut, only saying it was disgusting to lose to a damn old geezer that talked too much. Course he said this as they were leaving the table. Shakespeare just smiled. He had actually enjoyed the other two men. While playing they asked a thousand questions about what it was like in the Yellowstone trapping with Bridger and he loved to talk about those times. He was used to answering questions about Bridger even though a lot of other mountain men were as good or better than he was. Seems Bridger was the onliest one people wanted to hear about.

He decided to get a room and sleep in a bed for a change. He was trying to remember the last time he slept in a bed that was soft, but he couldn't. He paid his fifty cents to the clerk at the hotel for the room and ten cents for a bath. He made his way up the stairs and found his way to the room. It was small, but it was clean. He had just removed his belt with his knife and tomahawk when there was a knock on the door.

"Who is it?"

"Your bath, sir," replied a feminine voice from the other side of the door.

He walked over, opened the door and a young black lady slid a empty wash tub in the room. She then picked up a bucket of hot water and poured it into the tub.

"I'll be right back with another bucket," she said as she left. "Go ahead and get in."

This took Shakespeare by surprise, her telling him to get into the tub and she will be back with more water. He'd be damned if he was going to get naked and then have her come back into the room. It wasn't like he'd never been naked with a woman before because he had, but there's a time to be naked and then there's a time to be naked. This wasn't one of those times. He wasn't going to let his privates be seen by a perfect stranger. Hell, she couldn't be mor'n twenty years old. When she came back he was sitting on the bed. She didn't say anything, just poured the bucket of hot water in the tub, smiled and left, shutting the door.

Shakespeare took off his clothes and eased himself into the hot water but not before he had locked the door. He lay back and relaxed. He could probably count on his fingers the number of times he had actually had a hot bath in the last thirty odd years and by damn he was going to enjoy this one. Most of his baths had come in a cold mountain stream that shriveled him like a old prune.

Relaxed in the tub he thought about the men who had played cards with him. He had enjoyed telling the stories of him, Bridger, and Watkins and their trapping adventures. They seemed to enjoy them too. He was also glad the other young whippersnapper had decided to keep his mouth shut. He shut his eyes and slid farther down in the water.

"A shut uf gud wheskee wuld make this purfeet," he said out loud. He lay there a few more minutes thinking about Ben and his son. "Bet tha young'un is tall and thick jus like his pappy," he thought. "Probably blue eyed and good lookin' just like Ben." He stood up and dried himself off. He put his pants on, blew out the kerosene lamp and felt of the bed with his hand. It was soft and when he lay down, it was comfortable. However, after about thirty minutes of tossing and turning, he was still awake.

"Tha hell with it," he said, and threw the pillow and blanket on the floor and lay down.   He was asleep in five minutes.

~~~

With the first light of dawn, the coach was approaching Fort Inge. Yawning and wiping the sleep out of his eyes, Tye was ready to step out as soon as they stopped. He was getting up out of his seat when a familiar sounding voice broke the silence of the early morning.

"Ye two lovebirds in there by chance?"

"O'MALLEY!" Tye shouted. "Is that you?"

"Who else?" came the reply.

Tye sat back down and looked out the window at the craggily old face of Rebecca's guardian.

"What in hell's bells you doing here?"

"Orders, Mr. Watkins Orders." O'Malley replied.

"Orders?" Tye said. "What orders...and what the hell is that on your sleeve?"

O'Malley held his arm out so the new stripes could be seen by Tye and Rebecca. "The good Major seen fit to make me Sergeant Major O'Malley, what after my heroic action against old Tanza," he said laughing.

"I thought you should have had that rank a long time ago. Now, what's this about orders?"

"They were short and simple, Mr. Watkins. Let's see now, how did the good Major put it?" He stopped and scratched his chin, pretending to be deep in thought. "Oh, yeah. I remember now. He said I was to get your sorry ass back to Clark, pronto."

"What's the problem?"

"What else? Apaches are out again."

Tye stepped out of the coach and helped Rebecca down. Lieutenant Rogers stepped out behind Rebecca and shook Tye's hand and bowed to Rebecca. "Been my pleasure to ride with you."

"Pleasure's been mine Lieutenant," Tye replied. You just remember some of the things I mentioned and you'll be alright." Tye turned to O'Malley. "This young man," he said, nodding toward Rogers, "is Lieutenant James Rogers. Lieutenant, this is Sergeant Major O'Malley. He is Rebecca's guardian." They saluted each other, and then shook hands.

"I appreciate everything, Tye," Rogers said.

"You'll do fine, Lieutenant. You'll do fine. Maybe we'll meet again." They shook hands and the Lieutenant turned and headed toward headquarters.

"Getting younger and younger, ain't they?" O'Malley said. He nodded toward the troops. "You will find Sandy over there. He's saddled and waiting." Sandy was Tye's horse that was given to him by Major

Thurston for his part in bringing down the Vasquez gang a few weeks ago. He was a sorrel and big, strong, and fast. He had already proven his worth to Tye, having saved him once by alerting him to an ambush. A man, if he was smart, could learn a lot by knowing and watching his horse's actions.

O'Malley had brought an army ambulance along for Rebecca to ride in.

"Get a bed made in the ambulance for Rebecca and we'll be moving out. We could be there by nightfall," Tye said.

Tye walked over to where Sandy was standing. Sandy started snorting and stomping his feet when he recognized Tye. He nuzzled Tye's shoulder and then dropped his head for his usual scratching between the ears.

"Spoiled as a little kid, ain't he, Sergeant."

"Never saw a horse as fond of its master as that one, that's for damn sure," OMalley answered wistfully.

"Ain't it a shame," Tye said laughing.

Rebecca walked over to them and patted Sandy on the neck. She looked tired and her hair was a little messed up. She gave Sergeant O'Malley a big hug and a kiss on his cheek.

"One of the troopers is making a bed for you in the ambulance, honey." Tye told her. "I'm riding Sandy and we're going to try to get to Clark by dark. Let's get some breakfast and I'll have the lady make you something to take with you to eat later." He turned to O'Malley. "We'll be ready in twenty minutes."

Chapter III

After eating a hearty breakfast in the hotel's restaurant, Shakespeare had made his way to the stables and had saddled his horse and was tying the rope from his pack horse to his saddle when he heard a familiar voice.

"You enjoying my money you damn, stinking, old geezer?" Shakespeare, recognizing the voice of the loudmouth from yesterday, never turned around, continuing to tie the rope to his saddle.

"DAMN YOU! Look at me when I'm talking to you," the man hollered and grabbed Shakespeare by the shoulder and roughly spun him around. The stable boy came out to see what all the commotion was about.

"You took my money yesterday."

"Fare and squar, which is mo'rn I can say, fur yu."

"What are you talking about?"

"Yu're wun sorree poker player, sunny. Yu kuldn't win even deeling off tha bottom."

The commotion had drawn a small crowd now and everyone heard what was being said. Out here, most men played poker; most for money, others for

34

recreation and no one liked a cheat.

"You calling me a cheat?" The man screamed.

"I wached yu fur foer hours and if yu had been winnin, I bet tha uther men wuld have said somethang."

"DAMN YOU!" the man shouted as he backed up reaching for his pistol stuck in his belt. It was half way out when the Bowie buried itself in his chest. The gun went off, the bullet striking the ground and ricocheting into the wall of the stable. The man stood there for a second or two and then fell face forward, dead before he hit the ground. It had happened so fast no one in the crowd had a chance to move or say anything. They all came forward now and stood over the dead man. One of them was one of the men that had been playing poker yesterday.

"There's going to be hell over this, Shakespeare. His brother is the sheriff," the man said.

Another spoke up. "Was a fair fight. The man went for his gun. We all seen it." Yet another said, "Hell, the sonofabitch has been cheating for years. We all knew this would happen soo...".The man was spun around before he could finish by one of the largest men Shakespeare had ever seen.

"You going to say?" The big man growled at the man who was talking.

"N...Nothing, John... Nothing," the man stammered out. Shakespeare noticed for the first time the big man was wearing a star on his chest. All the people backed up as the man leaned down and turned the body over. He raised his head slowly and looked up at Shakespeare. Shakespeare knew he was in big trouble just from the look in the man's eyes.

"You just murdered my brother you sonofabitch!" The man reached out and grabbed

35

Shakespeare's buckskin shirt and threw him to the ground and then kicked him in the ribs.

"JOHN...JOHN..."a voice from the gathering crowd screamed. "Wasn't murder, John. Your brother went for his gun. This here feller killed him in self defense. We all seen it."

"Really now? You all seen it?" He bellowed in a threatening voice. "How about you, Jesse? You see it?" Jesse hung his head and kicked the dirt with the toe of his boot.

"How about you, Olson...you see it?" The man he called Olson hung his head, saying nothing.

"Anyone else here see what happened?" There was complete silence except for the shuffling of boots from the embarrassed men. "Didn't think so." He picked up Shakespeare by the collar. "You're gonna hang for killing my brother you old bastard!" and shoved Shakespeare toward the street... and jail.

Shakespeare saw the man who he had played poker with yesterday. "Take care of my horses for me, would you?" The man nodded.

That afternoon Shakespeare was playing checkers thru the bars with a young deputy. Everyone in El Paso had heard what had happened and felt sorry for the old man, including the deputy. The only problem was that no one was going to buck Big John. Shakespeare knew he was a dead man if he didn't do something quick. They were having his trial, if you could call it that, in the morning. The sheriff had left to go get something to eat and he figured it was now or never. As the young deputy reached to make a move, Shakespeare reached through the bars and with his hand behind the man's neck, slammed his head into the iron bars, knocking him out. Shakespeare held him while he removed the keys from the man's belt and then gently lowered him to the floor.

Unlocking the cell he quickly made his way to the desk and took his gun, knife, and tomahawk from the drawer. He also took the envelope that had his money in it. He took twenty dollars out and stuck it in the deputy's pocket.

"He's gonna need it cause tha damn shariff will problee fire him," he muttered as he made his way out the back door and to the stables. He found his horse still saddled along with his pack horse.

"Didn't figure they would hold a tough old codger like you," came a voice from the shadows. The man stepped out and it was one of the men from the card game yesterday...the man he asked to take care of his horses earlier.

"I figure you have about a half hour head start old timer. The sheriff will be plenty upset and he will chase you to hell if he has to. Good luck." He stuck his hand out and Shakespeare took it in a firm handshake.

"Thanks. I kan problee luse him on tha trail but thanks fur tha wurning." He mounted his horse and left town the back way, not down the street. He knew if the sheriff caught him now there would be no bringing him back, no trial... just a shooting... or a quick hanging.

~~~

The patrol, with Tye and Rebecca, could see the lights of Brackett shortly after the sun dropped behind the distant hills. Brackett was a small community of less than a hundred folks. It was located on the north side of the Old Mail Road and Fort Clark was on the south side. Only the Old Mail Road and Los Moras Springs Creek separated the two. The town's population was a mixture of Mexicans, trappers, buffalo hunters, a few merchants, and of course, the ladies that worked the two saloons. Besides the two saloons, there was a blacksmith, two stables, and one store that sold a little of everything from clothes, guns, ammunition, and food staples like flour, beans, coffee, etc. A small hotel and restaurant, The Sergeant, was the only place a man could get a bath, a room or sit down at a table and eat. There was no church and no school in the town. The town was founded shortly after Fort Clark was established in 1852.

The Fort itself, like most other forts in Texas, had no walls. It was bounded on the north and east sides by Los Moras Creek. The Fort was established here next to Los Moras Springs because it was not only the largest spring in the area but no one could ever remember it going dry, even in the driest of years. The water was clear, pure, and always cold. Construction of permanent buildings was going on at the Fort. Buildings made mostly of rock and mud would stay fairly cool in the blistering heat of the Texas summer and warm and snug in the winter. There was an abundance of oak trees, pecan trees, long grass, flowers, and plants of all kinds. It was like an oasis in the desert. For a hundred miles in any direction, one could find only the short grama grass, chaparral or mesquite, sage, cedar, and cactus of all kinds. It was a rugged and arid land that surrounded the oasis where the Fort was located.

As soon as the patrol arrived at the Fort, Tye took Rebecca to O'Malley's, and then he and O'Malley went to meet with Major Thurston. They told the ladies they would be back in a hour or so to eat. They took their mounts to the stables where they fed and watered them before heading to see Thurston. As soon as they had left, Mrs. O'Malley wanted Rebecca to tell her everything about their trip to San Antonio. They talked as they prepared the meal. It was all Mrs.

O'Malley could do to wait to spring the news of what the troops had done for the two of them while they were gone, but she kept her mouth shut. Everyone wanted it to be a big surprise.

Thurston was standing on the porch at Post Headquarters when he saw them coming. He returned O'Malley's salute and shook Tye's hand.

"Glad you're back, Tye," he said as they walked into his office. "We have a problem about thirty or so miles southwest of here." He walked over to the large wall map and studied it for just a moment before placing his finger on a spot just east of the Rio Grande River. "This is about where a family was supposedly killed by a band of Apaches led by a young buck by the name of Grey Owl three days ago."

Tye walked over to the map. "Mexican family by the name of Cobos?" Tye asked. Thurston took the cigar out of his mouth before speaking.

"That's the name given but it's not confirmed as of yet."

"Damn." Tye swore as he walked to the window.

"You know them?" Thurston asked. It seemed that Tye knew every settler and rancher within fifty miles.

"Not well, but good enough to know they were good people. Had a daughter and a son if I remember correctly."

I haven't heard back from the patrol I sent to investigate the story, and it worries me. I should have by now."

"Who did you send?" Tye questioned.

"Lieutenant Jackson," Thurston said. "And before you say anything about him being green, I didn't have a choice in sending anyone but him. Lieutenant Garrison and Captain Delacruz are still laid up from

39

wounds. Lieutenant Bennet is in the hospital sick. Lieutenant Benson is on patrol north of here and Lieutenant Cummings is on patrol south and east. Captain Henson is on leave and not due back for a week. I sent Sergeants O'Rourke and McCleary and your best scout, Williams with him. I also gave him specific orders not to engage with Apaches unless it was completely unavoidable. His orders were to locate the homestead and bury the victims, then find out what direction Grey Owl had gone, then report back to me."

"Who is this, Grey Owl?"

Thurston sat down in his chair before answering. "Young buck, maybe nineteen or twenty. He was related to one of the two men you killed at the crossing when you rescued the Turley kids. The scuttlebutt that's going around is that his one goal in life now is killing whites...especially one white man."

"Let me guess," O'Malley butted in. "Tye?" Thurston nodded his head.

"When do you want me to leave to find the patrol?" Tye asked.

"In the morning, if they haven't come in by then," Thurston replied.

"How many Apaches are loose, major?"

"Portably about twenty to twenty-five. But there's a report of another bunch that has left Fort Davis, headed south. By the way, the Comanche are raising hell as far south as Fort Stockton and Sonora."

"Don't the devils know they cannot win in a war against the Army?" O'Malley said, spitting into the spittoon.

"Sure they do," Tye replied. "Deep down, the older, wiser ones know. The young ones don't or at least they don't want to believe it. They want to live like their fathers did; free. They want to live the stories they have heard from their fathers and grandfathers. They are a prideful people and they will not be pinned up like cattle and be hand fed. I know they are not getting what food was promised them and that's the whole crux of the problem. If the agents were doing their job of keeping them content, our trouble with them would be cut in half. Like I said, they have a lot of pride and you are always going to have a few causing trouble. Let's hope those two groups don't meet up. That could be a disaster for the patrol." He turned to leave with O'Malley. "See you early, major."

~~~

Lieutenant Jackson had found the homestead the day before. The condition of the bodies made even the old veterans turn away. It was all Jackson could do to speak without losing everything on his stomach. They found two women stripped and spread-eagle on the ground, hands and feet tied to stakes driven into the ground. One was obviously the daughter. She looked to be about fourteen or fifteen years old. Both had surely been raped several times and then had their throats cut and scalped. The old man had to probably watch before they killed him. His was a terrible death as he was tied upside down on a wagon wheel and a fire set under his head. A boy of about ten or so was the lucky one; he had two arrows in the back and died quick. He had been scalped also. The heat and the buzzards had made a mess of the remains; eyes plucked out and stomachs ripped open with the internal organs eaten or spread on the ground where the ants were feasting. It was a disgusting, sickening sight.

"Sergeant O'Rourke!" Jackson hollered.

O'Rourke came running. "Yes Sir," he

shouted, saluting.

"Take some men and get the graves dug over there at the base of that cliff, to the left of the homestead."

"Yes sir." O'Rourke saluted and wheeled around, shouting some names of troopers to come with him.

Jackson turned and saw Sergeant McCleary. "Sergeant, get some blankets and wrap the remains so we can get them buried proper."

"Yes Sir, Lieutenant, right away."

"Williams," Jackson said to the scout. "Find out what direction the hostiles went and report back to me." With everyone busy following orders, Jackson walked over to one of the remaining walls of the homestead and lost his breakfast. He immediately felt better and went to where O'Rourke had the men digging the graves. They would be shallow because of the rocky land. He ordered three more men to gather rocks to put on the graves to keep the coyotes and other varmints from digging them up.

Not one of the men were aware of the twenty pair of black eyes that were watching their every move from a brush lined ditch, less than fifty yards away. Grey Owl gave a hand signal and three braves left to follow the scout. Grey Owl was anxious for it to be over with. He was confident of his success because the stupid bluecoats did not suspect they were close. No sentries had been posted. He was going to wait for the right time. Only six of his men had rifles but all had bows. They would all use the bow and arrow this time and conserve their bullets. If all went well, most would have rifles, pistols, and plenty of bullets in a few minutes.

The bodies, wrapped in blankets, were brought to the graves and lowered into them. As the men were gathered around the graves, heads bowed, they heard gunshots from the west. Grey Owl signaled for his men to release their arrows at the same time. As the soldiers turned toward the sound of gunfire, the arrows plowed into them. Jackson was hit in the side and started to shout an order but another arrow sliced into his throat. He drowned in his own blood. Only four troopers had not been hit with the first volley. The Apaches had released a second wave of arrows just as the first had struck their targets. This second wave took out all the remaining ones. Not all were dead but all were hit. An old corporal who had been hit tried to rally the men that were still alive around him but he died when the second volley of arrows hit.

Only four troopers remained alive and they panicked, and did the one thing you should never do. They surrendered to an Apache and expected mercy. There is no such word in the Apache language. Those four had the arrows viciously jerked from their bodies, and tortured unmercifully before they were killed. All the bodies of the troopers were scalped and stripped of everything useful. Only two of the three sent to get the scout returned. The scouts body was not mutilated a sign of respect for a fighting man. They rode off shouting, firing their rifles, and waving the scalps they had taken. They had guns, ammunition, food, and a new leader, Grey Owl. They were invincible.

~~~

Far to the north, Shakespeare topped a hill and dismounted. He had been traveling steady for four hours and knew his horses needed a rest. He had backtracked, used branches from the mesquite to wipe out his tracks, and had traveled almost a mile in a shallow creek trying to lose the sheriff and his posse. He scrambled to the rim and looked down on his back trail. He may be seventy plus but his eyes were still clear and he could see as good as a turkey buzzard, which was good.

"If'n I didn't kno better I'd beleev tha man is part Injun," Shakespeare mumbled disgustingly when he saw the cloud of dust the posse was raising about three miles back. He walked back to his horses and poured some water into his hat and gave both of them a drink. He knew they were tired so he flipped the reins over his saddle horse's head, catching them deftly in his hand and started walking, leading the horses. He looked at the sun and figured there was about three hours of daylight left. "I'll walk fur awhile an give them a gud blow," he thought to himself. He looked over his shoulder toward the direction of the posse. "Tha will gain sum ground with me walkin but tha will have tu rest their mounts befor long an mine shuld be fresh," he thought. "I'll put sum distence between us then."

~~~

Big John Rafferty, leading the posse, was in no mood for any slackers and was pushing the posse hard. Ross Rafferty, the man Shakespeare had killed, was his only kin and he wanted revenge. He was not listening to anyone about it being a fair fight. He wanted blood; Shakespeare's. The two men from yesterday's card game, Jess Faulks and Isaac Rosser, were in the posse. Like the others in the posse they were not anxious to catch Shakespeare. They had voluntarily joined the posse wanting to make sure Shakespeare made it back alive to stand trial if they caught him. The others were forced by the sheriff to be in the posse and Jess and Isaac knew it wouldn't take much for them to head back home. They all knew the situation. They knew Ross's mouth and card cheating would get him killed sooner or later, and none wanted to see a man who was defending himself railroaded by the dead man's brother. Then, none of them wanted to face the sheriff either. Jesse and Isaac hoped that sooner than later the men would all stand up to Big John at the same time.

~~~

Back at the fort, there was a feeling of friendship and love around the dinner table at the O'Malley's. By the time Tye and O'Malley returned from meeting with Thurston they just had time to wash up before the meal was on the table. Tye was sitting across from Rebecca, and next to the Turley kids. The kids had been staying with the O'Malley's since Tye had rescued them from Tanza. He knew that Mr. and Mrs. O'Malley had indicated they would love to raise them as their own. After a lot of thinking and talking with the children, Tye had made his decision.

As soon as they finished their meal, the children went outside to play. Coffee was served and the four of them sat at the table drinking it.

"I've given the welfare of the children a lot of thought," Tye said looking at the O'Malley's. "I think living with you two would be the perfect place for them." Tears of happiness welled up in Mrs. O'Malley's eyes, and she stood up and came around the table and hugged Tye's neck. Even the crusty old Sergeant choked up and could not speak. They hadn't had kids around for a long time and felt they needed the children as much as the children needed them.

Later, after the kids were put to bed, O'Malley

suggested they take a stroll along the creek. Tye rolled a smoke and O'Malley had his usual chew as they walked. When they rounded a bend in the creek, Tye stopped.

"That house wasn't here the last time I was along this creek."

"Maybe we have new neighbors," Mrs. O'Malley said. "Let's take a look."

When they stepped on the porch, Tye felt like he had been sucker punched. He stepped back, leaning against one of the post supporting the porch. Rebecca's mouth fell open and tears ran down her cheeks. Inscribed on the heavy wooden door was:

Built for Tye and Rebecca Watkins
By the troops of the Fourth Cavalry
September 1868

Tye stood on the porch, holding Rebecca, speechless.

"Damn, momma. First time since I met him, the boy has nothing to say," O'Malley said, laughing and holding his wife's hand.

"I...we..." Tye stammered for words. "Is this for real?" He finally got the words out.

"As real as can be," came a voice from the woods. Tye turned to see Thurston, Garrison, and several troopers he knew, approaching from where they had been waiting.

"I don't know what to say," Tye said.

"Hell, Tye. Don't say anything. You just keep saving our sorry butts like you been doing," one of the men said. Everyone laughed.

"Well, you two going to stand there like statues or are you going into your new home?" Thurston asked.

The main room was large, about twenty by twenty with the usual ten foot ceiling. There was a sink, cabinets, and cook stove along one wall. There was a table to dine on with four chairs. A couch and a rocker completed the furniture, except for a oval rug on the floor. Two doors led to bedrooms and all of Tye's and Rebecca's belongings were in the larger of the two.

The troopers brought out the beer for the men and tea for the ladies and they began to celebrate the occasion. A few minutes later the regimental quartet showed up and began singing the latest songs. It wasn't long before all were singing and having a great time. All too soon the party was over, and Tye and Rebecca were left alone in their new house. Standing on the porch under a beautiful Texas sky, they were holding hands.

"I can't believe they did this for us, and in a week," she whispered.

"I don't think I have ever been so shocked before in my life," Tye said. They looked at the inky black sky with its countless twinkling stars and back at each other.

"Let's go into our new home," Tye said as he picked her up and carried her through the door.

Chapter IV

Tye was sitting on the porch of headquarters well before daylight, waiting on Thurston. He was there for less than five minutes when the major arrived.

"Don't guess you heard from Lieutenant Jackson and the patrol?"

He could tell by the look on Thurston's face that he was stressed out. Thurston didn't say a word, only shook his head no. Tye got up and followed him into his office.

"I made out this requisition last night, Tye. I've made sure the quartermaster is there now. Take it and get what supplies you need for two or three days." He handed it to Tye. "Be careful," he added.

"Always am," Tye said smiling. "I'll be on my way in thirty minutes."

~~~

Shakespeare had walked until almost midnight. He was tuckered out and barely had the energy to take care of his horse's needs, namely water and oats, before lying down on his bed roll. He figured the posse made camp shortly after dark since the sheriff would have a hard time tracking him after dark. If they had, he had put some more distance between them. He thought about this country and wondered why in hell Ben had decided to settle down here. It was a far cry from the cool mountains of the Yellowstone or the high mountains of the Rockies. He reached into his shirt pocket and fingered the old, yellowed envelope... the letter he had received from his friend Ben and he cherished it as his most prized possession.

More than one friend had read it for him. He now had it memorized. It told of Ben's taking a wife, having a son, and asking Shakespeare to come down and live with them. Even had a map at the bottom with the location of his homestead. The letter was dated October 14th, 1845. It had taken over a year for it to catch up with Shakespeare. When it did, he promised himself he would make the trip. It took another twenty-plus years for him to actually make it. He had heard about Ben's death from a trooper that had been at Fort Clark before coming to Fort Bent in Colorado where Shakespeare was scouting. It was the same trooper that told him of Tye's reputation along the Border. He was now seventy one years old, no real home, no family he knew of, and by God he was going to see this here son of his friend. He fell asleep depending on his horses to alert him to anyone or anything coming close to camp.

~~~

Tye was a few miles west of Fort Clark on the Old Mail Road by the time the sun was peeking over the tops of the hills to the east. He knew a shortcut to where the Cobos's homestead was so he would not be following the patrols trail. He figured if anything happened, it would have been at the homestead or

49

close to it and his way would save three or four hours. He figured he would be there late this afternoon. He looked at the cloudless sky.

"Going to be a mite warm today Sandy," he said, leaning forward and scratching Sandy between the ears. Sandy shook his head and whinnied, causing Tye to smile. Sometimes he thought Sandy could understand everything he said. He stopped and rolled a smoke.

"I'll tell you something Sandy, I missed this while I was in San Antonio"... looking around at the arid landscape. "A lot of people think this country is terribly ugly, but to me, it's beautiful. Yep, I missed it." Sandy nickered. Tye reached down and patted him on the neck again. "I missed you too Sandy." He laughed at himself for talking to Sandy but he knew a lot of men who talked to their horses. Talking is as natural as breathing to a man and out here in Tye's line of business, he was alone a lot. Besides, if a man didn't let air out by talking, he might just explode.

He left the Old Mail road about noon and the terrain immediately became more difficult. It was impossible to go very far in a straight line because of ravines, hills, large boulders and thick stands of mesquite. The bleached rocks were reflecting the sun's rays and added to Tye's misery. Sweat was dripping from his face and neck and trickling down his collar, soaking his buckskin shirt that was sticking to him like a second skin. The shirt had been made years ago by his mother for his father. His father was wearing it when he was killed. It smelled of wood smoke and stale sweat. The shirt was well worn and had several places where holes had been sewn up such as the hole from the bullet that killed his father and two holes where Tye had been hit. One of the holes was from a bullet and the other, an arrow and several holes that had been cut in knife fights. The shirt would be with him forever.   It was part of him.

Squinting his eyes against the sun's glare on the rocky ground, he was alert to everything. He missed no bush, rock, or ravine where trouble may be lurking. This was done without him even thinking about it...it was natural to him, like breathing. He loved this life, this job, even as dangerous as it was. It was like his father always said...a man never feels more alive that when bad things could happen at any second.

It was getting hotter with every passing minute and only a few small, white clouds were moving across the blue sky every once in a while to temporarily block its burning rays. He was staying on the side of the hills, never on top where it might be easier traveling, because he did not want to be sky lined and easily spotted. He didn't travel on the canyon floor because that's where someone would be looking for tracks. He moved slowly and steadily.   Sudden movements could draw attention to anyone watching. He had no shiny objects on his person or his saddle that could reflect the sun. He even had the gold crossed sword emblem of the cavalry taken off the crown of his hat. He hadn't survived out here in this line of work for as long as he had by being careless or stupid.

Nothing was moving out here but a few rabbits, lizards, and the ever present damn buzzards that were always circling, waiting for something or someone to die. God, he hated them. He heard some birds chirping and turned Sandy toward the sound. Birds didn't usually get far from water so maybe there was a spring he didn't know about nearby. He knew most of the spring locations in this country but new ones are always popping up and old ones going dry. Knowing where the reliable ones were located could save a man's hide someday. He found the spring. It was a small one, more of a drip than anything else, but it was in an area that stayed shaded all day and water had collected in a small pool. He had plenty of water in his two canteens so he let Sandy drink his fill before moving on. He mentally recorded the spring's location for future use.

By late afternoon he was close to where the homestead should be. He crossed the patrol's tracks and suddenly pulled up Sandy when he saw a large flock of buzzards circling ahead.

'God, not again.' He thought to himself, remembering a few weeks earlier when he found the missing pay wagon and its butchered escort beneath a flock of these revolting creatures.

"My God!" He said a few minutes later when he entered the yard of the homestead, or what was left of it. The buzzards flew away reluctantly when he rode in. Bodies and body parts were everywhere. He tied Sandy to a mesquite upwind of the carnage so the smell would not make him skittish. He wet his kerchief and covered his face and walked into the nightmarish scene. It didn't take long for him to figure out what had happened. He walked west, away from the bodies and suddenly stopped. Staked out on the ground before him were the four men who had given themselves up. Stripped of their clothes, throats cut, scalped, and their genitals stuffed in their mouths. He shook his head, knowing the four had a long and painful death. He searched the perimeter and found the tracks leading west. He mounted Sandy, and began following them. He hadn't gone a mile when he pulled up. Several unshod tracks coming from the north had joined the ones he was following. He dismounted to study the tracks from the north. They were probably no more than twenty four or so hours old. He stood up and unconsciously was scratching

Sandy under the chin while looking west.

"Well, it looks like we have a real problem, Sandy. The twenty or so Apaches we were following may now be forty or more. If so, that spells a hell of a lot of problems for the folks living out here... and for you and me." He mounted Sandy. "Let's head back to the homestead."

He stopped at the homestead and managed to hold what little food that was in his stomach down. He gathered the bodies the best he could and placed them in the shallow graves that had been dug for the Cobos family. He then used a shovel he had found to cover them with a little dirt. He placed rocks on the graves to keep the creatures away. That would have to do till a burial detail could bury them proper. He picked up the bloodied Company C, 4th Cavalry banner, mounted Sandy, and headed back toward the Fort. He figured if he traveled all night he could be there by mid morning.

~~~

Shakespeare was dead tired when he lay down on his bedroll, but having lived the life he lived, he still woke up well before daylight, saddled up, and was moving south before the first gray streaks of dawn appeared. He was sure the posse was moving too. He wished he hadn't run his mouth so much during the card game in El Paso but then he had always been accused by his friends of running his mouth too much. He had talked about heading to Fort Clark to meet his friend's son. He figured this had gotten to the sheriff and maybe the sheriff wasn't as good at tracking as he had thought earlier. The posse was just traveling the general direction they figured he was traveling toward Clark.

In all his seventy-plus years this was the first time the law had been after him. Not that he had never broken the law because he wasn't sure of that. Where he had lived most of his life there was no law except the law of survival. He had avoided towns and people until the last fifteen or so years but even then he was staying at a Fort, not in a town. He was very familiar with military law but not the law that the civilians lived by. He knew he had killed that man in defense of his own life and the only reason he was being chased was the circumstances of the man being the sheriff's brother. Never being around town folks much, he certainly had never been on a posse. But knowing men the way he did, he figured they were mostly good folks and anxious to get back to their families. He figured it wouldn't take much to discourage them. The sheriff was a different story though.

~~~

When Tye arrived at Post Headquarters, he didn't bother to have the corporal announce him to Thurston. He walked straight by him and into Thurston's office.

"Tye!" Thurston stood up quickly. "What the hell you doing back here so soon?"

Tye threw the bloodied banner on the desk in front of him. Thurston stood there, frozen, staring at the banner. Finally, with a trembling hand he picked it up.

"Are they all...?

"Dead major," Tye answered. "Every damn one; including my scout."

Thurston slammed his fist on the desk. "I don't understand. I gave him specific orders not to confront the Apaches. I..."

"Wasn't his fault, Major," Tye said butting in.

Thurston raised his head up and looked at him.

"They were ambushed while burying the Cobos family.   Looked like they were cut down while standing around the graves.   Four gave up that weren't killed outright.   Their mistake...   It wasn't pretty."

Thurston sat down heavily in his chair and lay the banner on the desk in front of him.   He spread it out and smoothed it flat with his hands.   He then put his head in his hands with his elbows on the desk top. Tye understood his anguish at the death of his men. Tye had felt the same when men under his command, while he was with the Rangers, had been killed.   You wonder if there was anything you could have done to prevent it.   It takes time and a strong man, to understand and accept men dying under his command.   He doesn't like it, but accepts it.

"There's more bad news Major."

"MORE!" He shouted.   'How in hell can there be more?"

"I came across where another bunch from the north joined them, or at least, were following their tracks. If they got together, it's more than just a war party now.   They have over forty warriors and they are armed and feeling invincible.   Way too many for a patrol to handle.   I suggest you consider getting a large force together, maybe fifty men.   Let me find them and get this thing over with before more people are killed."

"Do you think the bunch is the ones from up at Fort Davis?"

"I'd bet a month's pay on it."

"It'll take most of the rest of today to get the paper work processed and the supplies together.   I'll have O'Malley pick the men and you should be able to

55

leave in the morning," Thurston said, getting up from his chair.

"Couple of other things, Major. I know how you feel about O'Malley. I feel the same way. I guess you know he and his wife are taking the Turley children to raise."

"So I heard," Thurston said. "I thought it very commendable of them."

"Well, those kids lost their parents; I would hate to see them do it twice."

Thurston scratched his chin, thinking. "I understand, Tye. I'll see that he is not going. He's sure going to be upset that he's not though. Now, what's the second thing you mentioned?"

"Would you check with the Apaches at their camp and see if they are receiving the food, and blankets that we promised them. I think a large part of the problem we are having is that damn agent, Taggart. He's making money besides what he makes from the government and we need to find out what and how he is doing it."

"I'll get on it as soon as I get everything together for this campaign," Thurston replied.

"Thanks, Major. I'll see you later today." Tye walked Sandy to the stables, gave him a rubdown and oats before going home to Rebecca. A man out here always takes care of his horse first, before taking care of his own needs... or seeing his wife for that matter. A horse out here was the most important thing a man could have on the trail. A fresh, well taken care of mount could mean the difference between living and dying sometimes. Tye would always take care of Sandy first. Course, a smart man wouldn't tell his wife that. Tye chuckled to himself at that thought.

When he approached the house, Rebecca, sitting on the porch, saw him coming and ran to him, throwing her arms around him. She pulled back suddenly.

"What are you doing back? I thought you were going to bring the patrol in."
He pulled her close to him, his arms around her tiny waist. "There's no patrol to bring in, honey. They are dead, every one of them." She looked him in the eye to see if he was kidding her. She saw he wasn't and fell apart.

"Oh Tye," she cried. "Evelyn's and Beth's husbands were on that patrol. Th...They are dead?" Tye nodded and she fell back against him sobbing uncontrollably. Next to Mrs. O'Malley, Evelyn and Beth were her best friends. Tye hugged her tighter.

"Let it all out, Rebecca. Let it all out." They stood there for a couple of minutes and Rebecca began to get control of herself.

"I...I need to go to them, Tye."

"Not yet, honey. They probably don't even know yet. I don't think you want to be the one to break the news to them."

She leaned against the gate and stared into space, seeing nothing, just staring.

"Did you actually see Jim and Les's bodies?" she whispered, turning back to him.

"I buried them with the others. I'm leaving with the troops in the morning to give them a proper burial and track the Apaches down that did it."

"Swear to me that you will come back to me. SWEAR IT!! "She begged loudly.

"Ain't nothing in this world could keep me from coming back to you, Rebecca, nothing."

He kissed her on the lips and tasted the salt from her tears. Her lips were warm, almost hot. She pulled away from him and looked into his deep blue eyes.

"I love you, Tye Watkins... I love you."

"I love you too, honey. And don't you fret over me not coming back. I always will. Before you came into my life, it didn't really matter whether I did or not. I've got a lot to live for now, so I'll be back. Besides, I'm too ornery not to." She kissed him and said she was going to see Mrs. O'Malley and tell her about the patrol.

"Are you coming with me?"

"Not this time. I rode all night to get back and I need a little sleep. I'll see you a little later." The last thing he wanted was to meet the wives of the dead men and have them ask him questions about how they died.

She kissed him on the cheek and left. He walked inside the house and over to the wash basin, stripped off his shirt and washed his face, hands, and neck. He walked over to the sofa, pulled off his moccasin boots and lay down. Almost immediately, he was asleep.

Chapter V

Thurston had a good office staff and the paper work had been completed much faster than he had expected. O'Malley was putting together a list of men for the campaign. Captain Delacruz was making sure the wagons needed to carry food, camp supplies, and ammunition was going to be ready. Captain McAlister, post surgeon, was responsible for the wagon with medical supplies. His assistant, Lieutenant Schuler, would accompany the troops on the patrol.

With everything being taken care of, Thurston, with a four man detail, was riding to the Apache camp to see the old chief. He had felt that the Apaches at the two camps were being cheated but hadn't spoken of it till Tye had. If it was true, he would personally kill that bastard, Taggart. No telling how many people had died in the last year, both red and white, because of the unrest in the camps and it was Taggart's responsibility to keep them pacified.

~~~

Tye woke up about two o'clock. He walked to

the wash basin and splashed some water on his face. He picked up the soap, lathered his face and quickly shaved. He pulled on a clean shirt and headed over to O'Malley's. Upon his arrival there, Mrs. O'Malley told him Rebecca was with her friends whose husbands had been killed. Tye told her to tell Rebecca he would be back in a couple of hours and headed to headquarters.

At headquarters, he was told Thurston had left to see the old chief at the Apache camp. Tye decided he needed a beer, so he walked across the bridge over Los Moras Creek and entered Brackett. He walked to the saloon where his friend, Jim, was the swamper, bartender, and owner.

When he entered the saloon, everyone wanted to buy him a beer. His mood darkened immediately when he saw Taggart, sitting at a rear table. Taggart had his usual white shirt on with a black string tie, black jacket, and black hat. He was a small man, five foot six or seven and weighed maybe one hundred forty pounds soaking wet. His face was long and narrow, with a protruding nose and small black eyes. He reminded Tye of a damn rat every time he saw him. Taggart looked like a little kid compared to the man sitting at the table with him. He was the biggest man Tye ever saw... and he wasn't fat. The mug of beer he held looked small in his giant hand, like a glass in a doll set little girls play with. He was also one of the ugliest men Tye had ever seen. He had thick black eyebrows over deep set eyes that appeared too small for a man of his size. His nose was wide, almost like an Apache's, and he looked like he couldn't smile if he had to. He had the look of a very dangerous man. Tye pushed his way through the men who wanted to buy him a beer and strode up to the table where Taggart and the giant were sitting.

"Taggart," he said loud enough for everyone to here. "You are a damn thief."

It was suddenly as quite as a tomb in the saloon and men were backing away.

"My good man, what are you talking about?" Taggart asked.

"I just came in from the field, Taggart, with a bloody Company C, Fourth Cavalry banner. That's all that was left of a patrol."

A low murmur went thru the crowd. Tye continued in a low, but firm voice that every man in the saloon could hear.

"It is your responsibility to keep the Apaches content, but you ain't. I don't think you are getting them the cattle, blankets, and other supplies they were promised. I think you are making money with the supplies and cattle they are not receiving. You are the reason the young bucks keep leaving and killing. You might as well have shot every homesteader and trooper that has been killed in the last year you sonofabitch."

With that, the giant stood up and with a low growl, swung a huge right hand at Tye's head. It would have caught most men flat footed but not a man with Tye's fighting experience and quick reactions. He ducked the huge fist and planted a tremendous right of his own on the big man's chin. It felt like he had hit a stone wall and the big guy didn't even blink. He caught Tye with a glancing blow to the cheek spinning him around and stunning him. He back peddled a couple steps and shook his head, clearing the cobwebs out. Full of confidence now, the giant moved in for the kill swinging a huge right fist. Tye ducked, and then planted a fist with all the power he could muster into the man's stomach. The air went out and the giant doubled over only to have his nose meet

Tye's knee that was coming up. He staggered backwards and placed his hands over his face trying to stop the blood. That was a mistake, as Tye hit him again in the belly. Air, blood and everything inside him came out in a rush and he fell to the floor, doubled up, groaning. Taggart had a horrified look about him. His face was pale, almost white, with all the blood having drained from it.

Tye turned his attention to the petrified man. He grabbed him by the collar and lifted him off the floor. Their faces were two inches apart when Tye started talking again.

"You get your thieving ass out of this area. We don't need your kind around here. On second thought, I ought to haul your sorry ass with me tomorrow to see the soldiers you killed. It would do you good to see them stripped, scalped, and their balls stuffed in their mouths."

A loud uproar went thru the crowd at that remark and then silence.

"My good man, you are mistaken. I..." Taggart never finished as Tye threw him about six feet thru the air and he hit the floor hard, spilling a spittoon all over him. A round of loud laughter went up, and then died as Tye walked over to the man who was on his hands and knees getting up. Tye kicked him hard in the butt and he sprawled again on the floor.

"Get out, Taggart. Get out or what them Apaches did to that patrol is going to be child's play compared to what I'm gonna do to you."

"TYE, LOOK OUT," a voice came from the crowd.

Tye whirled around to see the big man coming at him with a knife. Tye smiled at the man and motioned with his hands for him to come on. The man was huge and strong as a bear but he was not quick.

It took Tye about two seconds to realize this man was no knife fighter. Tye waited, not backing up, letting him come to him. He had drawn his Bowie from the sheath in the top of his right moccasin boot and held it low, in his right hand, edge up. The man struck a sweeping blow aimed at Tye's midsection just as Tye knew he would. Tye stepped quickly back and let the sweeping knife go by and striking with his own. His slicing blow cut the big man's knife hand above the wrist. With a yelp of pain, he dropped the knife and Tye was on him immediately. Tye had his Bowie at the man's throat, but had no intention of killing him, just scaring him. He swept the man's feet out from under him with his leg and threw the man to the floor. He turned back to Taggart but the man had fled like the stinking, cowardly, low life he was, leaving his partner to do the fighting.

"Somebody help this man get some medical attention," Tye said as he walked to the bar where his friend, Jim was. The crowd parted and there was a buzz in the crowd. Every man in the room knew Tye and of his reputation as a first class fighting man. Now, they had seen it close up and they were in awe of it. Not any two men would have stood up to the giant and Tye handled him like he was a boy. When he came at Tye with the knife, they thought they saw a look of pure enjoyment in Tye's face. They were talking in low voices as Tye got a beer from Jim. He was coming down from the rush that a man gets at a time like that, a time of anger or during a fight.

"Never liked that bastard, Taggart anyhow," he heard someone say from behind him.

"Sumbitch always acted like he was a little better than anyone else," said another.

"This place would be better off without his kind around," yet another chimed in.

"If what Tye said is true," came a voice from in the back of the room," we oughta just hang the bastard." Everyone was getting in their two cents worth now.

Men were coming over and patting Tye on the back. This fight would be talked about for a long time. As far as Tye was concerned, he was glad he was leaving early in the morning. He figured it hadn't been the smartest thing he had ever done... threatening and striking a government man and making accusations against him without proof of anything. But he sure did feel a hell of lot better.

~~~

At the Apache camp, Thurston had never seen such a sight. Half naked children running around looking like they hadn't eaten in a month; gaunt men and women with their suffering showing in their faces. Thurston also saw something else in their faces, a mixture of mistrust and hate. There were no dogs barking and he figured they had been eaten. He and his men, along with an interpreter, stopped in front of Two Tall's wickiup. No one dismounted yet. They would wait to be asked. A moment passed, and then Too Tall came out of his wickiup. Thurston could see how he got his name. He was six foot tall and thin as a rail, like everyone else. In his prime, he had to have been an imposing figure, as most Apaches were about five foot five to five foot nine. He motioned for them to dismount and sit. Thurston and Raines, his interpreter, sat across from the old chief and waited for him to speak first.

He uttered some guttural sounds that Thurston thought sounded part Mexican and part animal.

"He wants to know what you are doing here,

Major," Raines said.

"Tell him I heard he was not receiving cattle and supplies like he was promised and I came to see for myself." Raines translated Thurston's words and the chief became extremely animated...speaking loudly and holding up his fingers.

"The Chief says they receive only six or seven cows a month. They received blankets only once and not enough to go around. The corn and grain are never enough. Counting all the women and children, there's probably over three hundred Apaches in the two camps, Major. Seven cows a month ain't gonna cut it."

"That damn Taggart," Thurston cursed. "Tell the old chief he has my word that cattle will be here before the sun rises tomorrow."

He stood as his words were translated. He saw the chief nod his head and mumbled something.

"What did he say, Raines?"

"Another bluecoat lie," Raines said.

"Corporal Phipps, front and center," Thurston shouted.

"Yes Sir," Phipps answered as he came to where Thurston was.

"Phipps, ride to our herd and cut out a half dozen head of the biggest, fattest cows, and bring them here, pronto."

"Yes Sir, Major." He wheeled his mount around and was gone in a cloud of dust. Thurston and the rest mounted and headed out of the camp.

"Maybe if he sees I can be trusted, things will improve," he said to Raines.

~~~

Shakespeare had decided to try and help the

posse get discouraged a little quicker. It was a little over an hour before dusk and he was tired of looking over his shoulder, waiting for them to come riding in shooting at him. Sitting behind some shrub covered boulders on the rim above the canyon the posse would be riding through, he was going to scare them some. He was a good shot and his hands were still steady. He didn't want to hurt anyone, not even the sheriff but he had had enough of this running and hiding. He had been there almost a hour when they came into sight. The light was still good enough to be accurate. The sheriff was in front and the rest, seven of them, were strung out behind. When the sheriff was below him, he sighted in on him. It was going to be only a shot of fifty or so yards so he felt comfortable with it. He sighted the rifle on the crown of the sheriff's hat and slowly squeezed the trigger. There was no noise, not even a bird chirping...only the muffled sounds of the horse's hooves as they struck the soft sand of the canyon floor. The explosion of the sharps resounded off the rocky canyon walls. The sheriff's hat was blown off his head, men were hollering, horses rearing and bolting and there was chaos everywhere.

"ANYONE SEE WHERE THAT SHOT COME FROM?" Big John hollered from behind a large boulder he had quickly hidden behind. He had picked up his hat while scrambling to get behind the boulder and angrily crammed it down on his head. Most of the men had gotten control of their mounts except for the two who had been thrown. Only God knew where their mounts ran off to. No one answered the sheriff and it angered him even more. He was gonna kill this old man as soon as he saw him. As the men searched the canyon for the shooter another shot echoed thru the canyon and another one of the men's hat was blown off his head. They all saw the smoke and several shots were fired at the boulders where it came from.

As soon as he fired, Shakespeare was on the move to a position he had already picked out. He would be above and behind them now. He chuckled to himself.

"This heer will teech these tendarfuts not ta mess with us old geezers." He laughed again remembering the sight of the horses rearing, men hollering, men falling off their horses, and some of them crawling on their hands and knees to hide from him. Reaching the spot he had picked earlier, he carefully looked over the boulder. He saw that all the men's attention was where he had been. He chuckled again. "Wun mo shot shuld konvince them tha I ain't wurth all this."

He sighted in on one of the men's rifles that was being sighted in on the spot where he had been. He fired again and the man's rifle was knocked from his grasp. Shakespeare dropped back down and moved back to a spot in front of the men and fired again knocking another man's hat off. When it quieted down, he hollered.

"I'm tired uf this heer game boys. I kulda killed most uf yu by now but I'm not no killer. Eve'r damn wun uf yu kno I killed tha man in self defeense and yu have no bussness chasing me. This heer is yur last chance ta ride out uf heer. Tha nex time I site in on yu I won't miss."

He fired again and another man's rifle butt was splintered. He sprinted to his horse and quietly moved out. 'That oughta give them somethang ta think about,' he thought to himself. The sun was dropping below the hills as he headed south.

~~~

After rounding up the horses, the men assembled around Sheriff Rafferty. They were angry and shook up knowing how easily the old man could have killed some or all of them. Jess and Isaac were the first to speak their mind. They told Rafferty that they were tired of chasing a man who had no business being chased. Jess told him all the men were not going to take another step south. Rafferty was about to explode but was smart enough to know they were serious and no way he could force them without a fight and seven to one made the odds not in his favor.

"Okay. If that's what you want. Go crawling on your damn bellies back to El Paso. I thought you were men to ride the river with; guess I was wrong." He paused, looking every man in the eye before speaking. "When this is over and I'm back in town, don't a damn one of you ever...I mean EVER," his voice rising in anger, "come to me for help cause you sure as hell won't get it. Now get the hell out of my sight." He abruptly turned and walked to his horse, mounted up, and headed out.

"I hope he doesn't catch that old man," the man said whose rifle Shakespeare had just busted.

"That, gentlemen, will never happen. In case you didn't know it, he's chasing a man that is one third white man, one third Indian, and one third mountain lion. Rafferty has never seen the day he could out shoot, out fight, or out smart ole' Shakespeare," Jess said while mounting his horse. "Let's go home." Inside, he wished he could have seen that old man in his prime. "That would have been a sight," he said to no one in particular.

"What are you mumbling about?" Isaac asked.

"Nothing important, Isaac; just thinking out loud."

~~~

The night passed quickly; all too quick when Tye was with Rebecca, and a hour before daylight found him at the post stables. All the men were there and Tye was impressed with the sight. Fifty men and horses and four wagons full of needed supplies was a sight. Tye figured they would be strung out for at least two hundred yards, maybe a little more. That was okay for now but when they got into Apache country, being strung out like that wasn't too smart. He hoped they would have no trouble until they got about fifteen or so miles from the Apache Rancheria on the Rio Grande, where he figured the Apaches were. It was the camp that Tanza had used before and where Tye found him and killed him. He found the Turley kids there. It was a camp that looked to have been used for a long, long time.   The terrain would not let the wagons get closer than the fifteen miles, so they would set up a base camp with a hospital.   He figured Delacruz would leave eight to ten men to protect it from a surprise attack.

The troopers mounted and rode out by the twos, backs straight, shoulders square; looking like they were on parade instead of going into harm's way.   The Flag and the company banners were snapping in the early morning breeze.   Thurston stood at attention, holding his salute until the last man had passed. It always did something to his insides to watch his men ride out, uniforms clean, buttons shinning, sabers' rattling in their saddle scabbards, and the Flag...the Flag of the United States of American flapping in the wind always stirred his emotions. He knew a lot of them personally and he knew some of them would come back laying across their saddles instead of sitting in them.

"Protect them God. Protect them and have mercy on their souls," he whispered.

Tye felt good about the men O'Malley had assembled. There were forty enlisted men, Captain Delacruz who was in command, Lieutenants Garrison and Gorman, Sergeants O'Rourke, Anderson, and McKlesky. Also, there was Lieutenant Shuler, the surgeon. Tye had picked three of his best scouts, Billy August, Billy's younger brother, Dan, and also Lester Goodwill, to help him. He knew some of the others from previous patrols especially Corporals Phipps and Arnold. They had been with him when he brought in Alex Vasquez. Also with them was Corporal Ronald Christian who had actually saved Tye's life about a year ago in a fight with some bandits. "Fifty fighting men," Tye thought to himself. "Fifty good fighting men." He felt good about things as they rode out; even the air smelled fresh with the heavy dew they had during the night.

Chapter VI

Mid morning found the men several miles west of Fort Clark, traveling on the Old Mail Road. Tye and Billy were a quarter mile out front with Dan and Lester, each with a trooper, were a couple hundred yards on either side as out riders. They would keep the column from a surprise attack coming from the side. Tye was keeping the column as tight as possible. Stragglers would be easy pickings for the Apache. Tye wasn't worried about Apaches right now; but the men might as well get used to the way things were going to be. This was a veteran group for the most part. Men who knew what to expect on a campaign like this; heat, hunger, thirst, and the frustration of chasing an invisible enemy. Invisible that is, until he decides not to be. When that time comes... troopers usually die.

Captain Delacruz was a capable officer as far as Tye was concerned. He had scouted for him on several patrols and he had always been open to Tye's suggestions. Lieutenant Garrison was young but he had been with Tye when they brought down the Vasquez gang and he was steady and capable. He had been wounded in that fight and was not 100% but says the wound will not be a problem and convinced

Thurston he could handle it.

Delacruz was thinking about ordering a break when he saw Tye and Billy waiting on them about a hundred yards out. When the column arrived to where the scouts were waiting, Tye made the suggestion of a break to Delacruz, telling him this is where they turn off the road and the terrain will become much more difficult before long and they need the horses fresh. Delacruz nodded his head.

"I was thinking the same thing. Lieutenant Garrison," Delacruz shouted without turning around.

"Behind you sir," Garrison replied.

"Pass the word we are taking a thirty minute break."

"Yes, sir."

The men immediately started dismounting. Tye was watching. He wanted to confirm what he figured he already knew. Sure enough, every man loosened the girth on his mounts saddle, gave them water and oats before he took care of his own needs. Tye smiled. There wouldn't be much reason to give a lot of stupid orders. These men knew what was expected of them, and they would do it.

Delacruz had just sat down when Tye walked over to him.

"We have a slight problem, Captain."

"What kind of problem, Tye?"

"Take a look to the southwest at those clouds. I've been watching them and they are going to be here damn quick and it's going to be nasty."

Delacruz, upset with himself for not seeing them, "I should have noticed them myself. What do you suggest we need to do?"

"The storm will coming in from the southwest. Billy and me will look for a hill that has a vertical wall that runs north and south. If we can, we might be able to escape the main force of the storm. We'll leave now. You might consider cutting this break short or we're going to get wetter than hell."

"Get going then. We'll be five minutes behind you," Delacruz said. As Tye and Billy left, Delacruz was telling the men why the break was going to be shorter than planned.

They had gone about a mile when Tye saw the Apache. He had made a mistake and sky lined himself and was remaining perfectly still hoping he would not be seen.

"Billy," Tye said in a low voice.

"I see him. Must be a young buck; sky lining himself like that." They had to detour around a couple of big mesquites and lost sight of the Apache for just a second. When they looked again, he was gone.

"Best be extra careful, Billy," Tye commented.

Billy nodded and then pulled his mount up.

"There," he said pointing with his rifle.

Tye looked where he was pointing and saw a high cliff that looked to run north and south. It was a good half mile or so away.

"Wait here on the column, Billy. I'm going to take a look at that cliff." As he started toward it, he heard the distant rumble of thunder, and lightning could be seen in the western sky. Tye studied the clouds for a moment.

"Sandy, this is going to be a hell of a storm," Tye said patting him on the neck. When he arrived at the cliff, he could not believe what he saw. It was perfect. If they had looked for a year, they could not have found a better place to hold up. The face of the cliff was almost vertical, angling out at the top. The top would serve as a porch.

"Hell Sandy, we may not even get wet at all here." The cliff was about seventy-five feet high and maybe a quarter of a mile long. A cut in the wall about forty feet wide and sixty foot deep would be perfect for the horses. They may get a little wet, but the wind would not reach them. He looked back down the trail and saw the column, with Billy in front, about a half mile away coming toward him. He was gathering wood when they arrived. He immediately had his scouts gathering wood with him before the rain soaked it making starting a fire difficult.

"This place looks fine." Delacruz said

"Yes Sir. We may not even get wet." Tye said pointing to the overhang above them. The wind was up and the cool air that precedes a storm was making its presence known. The lightning was continuous now and the thunder was deafening. A minute later, the bottom fell out. It was raining as hard as Tye had ever seen it rain out here and with the wind, it appeared to be coming down horizontally. The overhang protected them and if you stayed fairly close to the face of the cliff, you never got a drop on you. Three fires were blazing and the aroma of coffee boiling replaced the smell of brimstone from the heavy lightning that was flashing everywhere. It was a terrific storm but from where they were, it was actually pleasant. It was cool, it was dry, and the coffee was good... as was the company.

"Saw an Apache about an hour ago, Captain," Tye stated.

"Apache!" Delacruz exclaimed; "Where?"

"About a mile back; probably a young buck cause he let himself be sky lined."

"Don't guess we're going to surprise them now," Delacruz said, looking off in the dark.

"Like I've said before, Captain, I don't think the army has surprised the Apache very many times. They always seem to know where we are. Sometime,

I think the hawks, crows, and every other creature talks to them, letting them know where their enemies are."

Tye walked over to where the horses were. He saw an old friend, Corporal Phipps, looking at them also.

"Humdinger of a storm ain't it, Tye."

"Sure right about that, Phipps," Tye replied, shaking the Corporals hand. He knew Phipps from previous patrols. Phipps was instrumental in helping Tye put an end to the Vasquez gang. He was a good soldier and Tye considered him a friend.

"I'm glad you're along, Phipps. I know where to come if I need a volunteer." Both men laughed. It was a private joke between them. Seems that when Tye had needed a couple of volunteers to track down Alex Vasquez, Sergeant O'Malley told Phipps that Tye had requested him personally for the dangerous mission. He found out later that Tye didn't and O'Malley had told Tye that Phipps and another man, Del Arnold had volunteered. Both were good soldiers and, as Tye's pa would say, were men to ride the river with.

Sandy made his way over to Tye for his head scratching. He nuzzled Tye's shoulder and dropped his head. Tye started his usual scratching.

"Got him trained like a puppy, don't you?

"I ain't to sure who has who trained," Tye said chuckling. "See you later, Corporal." Tye finished scratching Sandy and headed back to his fire.

Raucous laughter was coming from the fire about thirty yards from where Tye, Captain Delacruz, Lt. Garrison, Lt. Gorman, and the three scouts were drinking coffee.

"Must be some powerful war stories going on over there," Delacruz commented.

"Those 'war' stories probably are about their conquest in the rooms above the saloons in Brackett,"

Garrison added.

"Some of those encounters can be vicious," Gorman said laughing.

"How do you know?" Garrison asked.

"Wouldn't know personally, just heard about them," Gorman said with a straight face.

"Yeah, right!" Tye said, laughing as was everyone else.

Delacruz stood up and told Lieutenant Gorman to make the rounds and make sure everything is secure for the night. He turned to Garrison. "You have the sentries set for the night?"

"Yes Sir, and double on the horses," Garrison said.

"Good," Delacruz said rubbing his hands above the fire. "Damn chilly ain't it."

"Probably had a hailstorm close by," Tye said. "Think I'm gonna turn in. See you early, Captain."

"I'll be turning in too, as soon as I hear from Lieutenant Gorman that everything is well," Delacruz replied.

Tye nodded and lay down on his bedroll. His saddle served as a pillow and the wool blanket felt good as he pulled it up to his chin. Billy and the other two scouts had already turned in and one was raising the dead with his snoring. Tye raised up, saw the culprit was Dan. He picked up a small stick and tossed it, hitting him in the forehead.

"What the hell!!" Dan hollered as he sat up.

"How about staying awake long enough for the rest of us to go to sleep," Tye told him.

"How's my being awake going to help you go to sleep?" Dan asked, rubbing his forehead.

"No one can go to sleep with you snoring the way you do," Tye said laughing and lay back down. He was tired and was asleep in a few minutes.

Lieutenant Gorman reported back. "Everything is secure, Sir."

"Good," Delacruz said. "Get to your bedroll and turn in, Lieutenant. Going to be a long day tomorrow."

Within a few minutes, the only sound from the camp was the snoring of tired men, the footfalls of the sentries as they paced back and forth, and the occasional whinny of one of the horses. The rain had slowed to a drizzle now and the thunder was only a distant rumble. The camp had settled in for the night.

~~~

Grey owl was sitting in his wickiup at the Rancheria by the Rio Grande. It was the same Rancheria where Tye had found and killed Tanza and rescued the Turley children. It was the same Rancheria that Tye was headed for now. Grey Owl was content for now. He had killed many bluecoats two days ago and had not lost but one man. Each of his followers that left the reservation with him had guns now, and plenty of bullets for them. The men would do what he wanted for he was thought to have good medicine. They figured only one who was looked upon favorably by the great spirits could have led them to such a great victory. He was not so bold to think that the men would follow him forever. Apaches were superstitious as was all Indians of all the tribes. If a battle was lost, the leader was generally thought to have 'lost' his good medicine and another was usually elected.

With the warriors from the north joining him, he had more than four times the number of fingers on both hands. They were all young and most had only limited exposure to warfare. Their strength came from a burning hate for the 'Pinda-lickoyee', or white eyes, that flowed through each of their veins. They knew they could not stop the flow of the white man into their land but they wanted to live as long as they could as their fathers had...free. They would kill Pinda-lickoyees as long as blood flowed thru their veins.

Grey Owl hated them but he hated one above all others. The scout Watkins, killer of his father's brother, Lone Wolf and his friend, Tanza, was at the center of this hate. He intended to kill him himself. The killing would start tomorrow, but for now he just wanted to enjoy his status among the warriors. If things went wrong, that status could change by this time tomorrow. It had always been that way with the Apache, and he accepted it.

~~~

Tye was the first one awake. He shook out his moccasin boots and pulled them on. He strapped on his gun belt, took out his pistol and wiped it clean. He then took out each bullet and wiped them off and replaced them in the gun and holstered it. He took out his Bowie from the sheath in his boot and rubbed the blade back and forth on a rock to make sure it was razor sharp. He finished his daily ritual by cleaning his rifle. This all took about five minutes. His pa always told him you could have the best weapons in the world but they weren't worth a tinker's damn if they didn't work. He had been a fanatic when it came to his weapons and it rubbed off on Tye.

He stood up and walked over to the coals from the fire last night. Some were still glowing, so he placed a few small pieces of mesquite on them and fanned them with his hat. He had a nice fire going in a few minutes and soon had water boiling. He dropped in a handful of coffee grains. The aroma filled the early morning air quickly. Men started stirring about and Tye smiled. The only thing that would wake a horse soldier quicker than the aroma of fresh coffee was the sound of an Apache charge.

By the time the coffee was ready, Captain Delacruz and Lieutenants Garrison and Gorman made their presence known. Even old sawbones, Lieutenant Schuler, was there with his tin cup held out to be filled.

"Amazing how different this country smells after a good rain," Delacruz stated his head turned toward the black sky, sniffing the air.

"The landscape will look a little different today, too," Tye added.

"What do you mean, different?" Lieutenant Gorman inquired between sips of coffee.

"Greener," Tye answered. "All the dust will be off the plants and everything will be a little different color than yesterday."

Garrison sipped the scalding coffee, careful not to burn his lips on the infamous tin cup that was famous for that very thing. "When did it stop raining?"

"Little after midnight," Tye answered.

Tye was watching the men while sipping his coffee and noticed they were staring at the fire for no reason.

"Got a tip for ya'll. Might save your sorry butts sometime," Tye said.

Each man looked up at Tye.

"What's that?" Gorman asked.

"Staring into the fire can get you killed. If something happens, it takes a second or two for your eyes to adjust; could be the difference in living and dying."

"Never thought about that before; Makes good

80

sense though," Delacruz said. "I'll remember it." He turned to Lieutenant Gorman and Garrison, "Inform the sergeants that we will move out in twenty minutes."

"Yes Sir," came the reply in unison and both saluted, turned and left.

The troopers were not recruits and each knew what to do and what was expected of them. They, in turn, knew what to expect on a patrol like this, and they accepted it. There would be long days under blistering sun; never enough water; always the threat of sudden death. Seldom was the army beaten by the enemy, it was beaten by a merciless land that was unforgiving.

The column was ready in fifteen minutes. Tye and his scouts took their positions out front and to the sides as the column moved out.

~~~

Shakespeare had covered a lot of miles yesterday and slept well last night. He was now in the mountains and he figured close to Fort Davis where he would stop long enough to replenish his supplies.

'So this heer is wha Texcans kall montans.' He laughed at the thought as he looked at what he considered hills. "Sho as hell not like tha Yelleeston or Kolorado is it, Henree?" He said, reaching down and patting his horse on the neck. "No sir. These heer montons won't win no beautee kontest, tha's fur sure."

He had not seen anyone on his back trail since he fired at the posse. He was covering as much ground as possible, not worrying about them for now. He was looking for trouble though. He had cut enough sign to know there was more than a few Indians around. He didn't know the tribes around here but figured they were like the ones he had fought all his life in the mountains...mean, sneaky, and hell on wheels in a fight. It was getting dark quicker in the mountains than on the plains where he had been. He figured it was time to look for a place to hole up for the night. He found it a few minutes later. One hundred feet above the trail was what looked like a cave.

He made his way up to it, having to lead the horses. Tying them to a small cedar, he walked into the cave to look around. Satisfied, he led the horses in, unsaddled Henry and removed the rack off the pack horse. He gave them some water and oats and took them a little farther into the cave and hobbled them. With only a little light left, he went back down to the trail and carefully wiped out any sign of them heading off the trail. He even backtracked about a hundred yards wiping out tracks. It was darker than sin when he entered the cave again. He piled up some rocks in a circle to hide the small fire he planned to build. He hadn't had coffee in two days and he was needing some bad.

After the coffee was made, he walked to the cave opening and sat down, looking back along the trail he had been on.

"I be dammed," he said, looking at a flickering fire about a mile or so away.

"Tha has ta be tha damn possee. No lokal or Injun wuld make a fire tha big."

He was watching the fire when a horse's whinny startled him. He immediately rolled back away from the opening and making his way to his horses where he stood between them and with their heads on each side of him, clamped a hand on each of the nostrils. He figured no one was out after dark except someone looking for trouble and he didn't want a snorting horse making his presence known. He waited for five minutes before letting go and making his way back to the opening to take a look. He could see or hear nothing. He waited for ten minutes then went back and lay down on his bedroll. It didn't take him long to fall asleep.

Chapter VII

The column had covered three miles in the rough terrain by the time it was full light. Tye reminded Billy for the tenth time to be extra alert as he had one of those feelings that something was going to happen, and quick. He had told both Garrison and Gorman to make sure the men stayed alert and didn't doze in the saddle. It was easy to do in the heat and with the rocking motion of a walking horse. To counter this possibility, the lieutenants had their men trotting their horses when possible. Their rifles were out of the saddle scabbard, pointing skyward with the butt resting on their thighs. They were ready for trouble. He had reminded the captain and lieutenants of the old Apache trick of showing a few warriors to get an unsuspecting officer to chase them into an ambush. He hoped he had covered most of the things he expected to be possible happenings, but with the Apache, new things come up again and again.

The terrain they were in now was getting more dangerous by the mile. Deep arroyos, huge boulders, steep hills and canyons with walls covered by sage and cactus, all led to possible ambush sites. Tye felt it was time to set up a base camp as the wagons were having trouble making headway. He had found a suitable spot for the wagons and waited on the column and Captain Delacruz to catch up. The only drawback was a low hill about a hundred yards to the east where an Apache sharpshooter might hide. Tye figured to park the wagons between the hill and where the men would be. That would offer some protection if the situation arose. There was a gulley about thirty yards long and twenty yards wide that would be perfect for holding the horses.

When Delacruz and the column arrived, Delacruz spurred his mount up to where Tye was.

"Problem?" He asked Tye.

"No problem, Captain. I think it's time to consider making a base camp. It's going to get rougher on the wagons the farther we go. This is a pretty good spot."

Delacruz stood up in his stirrups, looking in all directions. "What about that hill over there?"

Tye was pleased that the Captain had noticed. A lot of officers would not have been so observant. "We can park the wagons between the gulley and that hill. It should offer enough protection."

Delacruz looked around one more time and then turned in his saddle to speak to Garrison.

"Lieutenant, Please notify Lieutenant Schuler that he will set his hospital up here. Pick eight men to stay here with him. Sergeant Anderson, bring Lieutenant Gorman to me."

"Yes Sir?" Gorman said when he arrived.

"Lieutenant, I want you to make sure each man has thirty rounds for his rifle and that each belt is full for his sidearm. Each man will have three days rations for himself and oats for their mounts. Have Sergeant O'Rourke stay here. He will be in charge of the camp."

85

"Yes sir, anything else, Sir?"

"No...carry on, Lieutenant," Delacruz ordered.

The more Tye was around Delacruz, the more he liked and respected him. He hadn't seen him in a battle situation yet, but he would bet this month's pay he would be just as cool and in control as he is now.

"How far are we from the Rancheria?" Delacruz asked Tye.

"No more than ten or twelve miles as the crow flies. Bout twenty- five the way we have to go," Tye answered. "It's going to be the roughest twenty- five miles you have ever traveled... boulders the size of houses, arroyos fifty to hundred feet deep, hills with sides so steep the horses will have to be led up and down them, and on top of that, the threat of an Apache ambush every step of the way."

They were on their way again within thirty minutes. Sergeant O'Rourke and the eight men were left with Lieutenant Schuler at the camp. Tye and Billy were in front about a quarter of a mile with the other two scouts, Dan and Lester, about a hundred yards to each side, accompanied by one trooper each. Without the wagons and the men left at the camp, the column was strung out less than half of what it was before. Tye told Delacruz it would be a good idea to keep the men riding very tight together and the ones in back had better stay sharp.

Tye was scouting the terrain carefully. Every sense was fine tuned. He would stop, check for any sign of trouble with his eyes and ears, and then move on another short distance before repeating the scenario. The hair on the back of his neck was bristling like it always does when trouble was brewing. It was nerve racking work and the sweat was running down both Billy's and Tye's face and neck, soaking their shirts. The sweat sure wasn't all from the heat either.

Delacruz was watching the two carefully. Not only was he watching for any sign from them alerting him to trouble but admiring their courage. He and every man knew the scouts would be the first targets and they had a tremendous amount of respect for what they did. Personally, Delacruz thought such a man had to be a little crazy to do it. He pulled up sharply and held his hand up to stop the column as he saw Tye give him the same signal. He watched as Tye and Billy was discussing something.

"You got the same feeling I have regarding that canyon ahead, Billy?" Tye asked.

"Yep," Billy replied. "If I was an Apache, that's sure as hell where I'd be."

Tye sat there, hands on the pommel of his saddle, studying the canyon. "Stay here Billy, I'll check it out."

"Let me do it, Tye."

"You sure that's what you want to do?" Tye asked.

Billy nodded and kicked his horse and moved toward the canyon. Tye heard a horse coming behind him and looked over his shoulder. Delacruz and Sergeant McClesky were coming to meet him. He turned back to watch Billy as he entered the canyon.

The sweat was pouring off Billy as he stopped at the canyon's entrance. He studied the sides carefully and wondered if maybe he should have let Tye do this. Entering the canyon, he could feel the eyes on him but he could see no sign of trouble. He was about half thru the canyon when he saw it. A glint of sunlight reflected off something. He stopped, took a long look, and slowly turned his horse around and backtracked the way he came in. He was moving slowly. He was a dead man if the Apaches thought he saw them. When he reached the mouth of the canyon, he slapped the rump of his horse with the rifle and was racing back to where Tye waited, grateful he hadn't been shot.

"Whatcha think, Billy?" Tye asked as Billy returned.

"They're there all right."

"Did you see them? Delacruz asked.

"No...but they are there," Billy said. "Think I saw a reflection of sunlight for just an instant." He looked at Tye. "I could feel "em, Tye."

"You think you saw...you felt them being there...how can you say they are there if you didn't see them?" Delacruz asked, somewhat confused. "That's pretty damn...."

"Go ahead and take your men thru that canyon, Captain, if you don't want to listen to us," Tye interrupted.

"I didn't mean it that way, dammit," Delacruz said. "But how can you say for certain they are in there if you saw no one?"

"Captain, men like us have a side to them most men don't have. We have a sense of feeling trouble. Only way a man in our profession can survive is to have it," Tye answered.

"What do you suggest we do then?" Delacruz asked.

"I'm thinking on that, Captain. I'm thinking on it," Tye replied. "Why don't you bring the men on up here, Billy?"

Tye took out the makings and rolled a smoke. Delacruz watched and was amazed Tye's hand was as steady as it was, considering the situation. Himself, he was nervous as a whore in church and wasn't about to try rolling a smoke even though he would love to have one.

~~~

Grey Owl was watching Tye's every move with the glasses that see far. He had taken them from the officer of the patrol he had killed three days earlier. He felt he could almost reach out and touch the hated scout. He was sure his trap was going to work and the white warrior's scalp would be hanging from his rifle by nightfall. He was delighted when six more warriors had shown up today. They were not Lipan like himself, but Kickapoo Apaches. One or two more victories and they would be flocking to him like buzzards on a carcass. His name would be mentioned with the likes of Cochise, Nanah, and Junah, in all the Apache rancheros.

He had enough warriors in the canyon, half on each side so when they opened up on the patrol, they would have the blue coats pinned down. The remaining warriors would charge from the canyon opening and over run the bluecoats from behind.   All this would happen after he shot the scout, Watkins. He figured the bluecoats would be lost without him telling them what to do. It was a good plan and should work. He wasn't impressed by the bravery of these bluecoats in his encounter with them at the homestead of the dead Mexicans.   It was going to be a good day, another great victory if the Great Spirit saw fit; if not... it was a good day to die.

~~~

Shakespeare had made his way back down to the trail and turned south when he heard the shots. He immediately knew who was in trouble. He figured it served them right and continued on his way. He went about ten steps when he stopped. More shots could be heard. "Dammit ta hell," he said disgustingly and tied his horses to some sage and starting back down the trail at a fast trot.

~~~

Back at the fort, Major Thurston was listening to the complaints of one James Taggart.

"That wild man should be in jail for what he did to me," Taggart said loudly. "Men can't go around punching, kicking, and threatening a government employee."

Thurston was both concerned and amused. Concerned that Tye had kicked the hell out of an employee of the Federal government; and made wild accusations about him to others. Amused that he wished he had been there to witness the ass kicking. He knew Taggart was a snake. 'I'm going to prove it somehow,' he said to himself.

"I will look into this matter myself when the patrol returns," he promised Taggart. When Taggart had left, Thurston picked up his hat, walked out of headquarters and across the bridge into Brackett. He decided to see Tye's friend, old Jim the bartender. If anyone knows everything about everything, it was a bartender or a barber.

~~~

Young Lieutenant James Rogers was on his first patrol out of Fort Inge. He was an observer as Lieutenant Franks was in command. It was as Tye had told him it would be. A day or two learning the fort's routine and then on patrol to learn the terrain. Lieutenant Franks seemed like a good officer and the men liked him. He had already figured out what Tye said was true about shave tail lieutenants. For the most part, they weren't too popular with the men.

Seems the arrogance of some had gotten a lot of good men killed unnecessarily in the past. No one wanted to go on a patrol with a lieutenant on his first patrol. He had heard the rumor, or was it just a rumor, that on occasion, an arrogant lieutenant had been shot and killed when leading a charge... from behind.

"That's not going to happen to me," Rogers thought to himself. I will ask questions and accept opinions before I do anything.

"You okay Lieutenant?" Franks asked.

"Wh...What. Oh yeah, I'm fine," Rogers replied.

"Looked like you were in another place," Franks added.

"Sorry. I was just thinking how anyone or anything could live, or want to live out here."

"I was the same way six months ago. This land will grow on you Lieutenant. At first, it's a barren, arid land. Then, you realize that it's full of life; plants, animals, and humans that have adapted to it. Before long, you start seeing a beauty to it that wasn't there before. I've grown to appreciate it for what it is.

They were silent for a moment before Franks spoke. "I hear you were in the coach with Tye Watkins when you were coming here."

Rogers nodded his head. "Yes, he and his wife."

"What did he look like?"

Rogers rubbed his chin for a second before speaking. "I figure him to be six two or three and maybe two hundred pounds. No fat on him. He has black hair that's almost to his shoulders, and blue eyes that go right thru a person when he looks at 'em. He is an extremely good looking man and moves with the grace of one of those large cats you see in side shows. On top of that, he is extremely friendly. His wife is the most beautiful lady I have ever seen."

"Six two, huh," Franks said. "I figured from his reputation, he had to be seven feet at least," he added smiling.

Franks pulled up suddenly and held his hand up. The ten men behind him stopped just as suddenly. The scout was coming back to them and he was in a hurry.

"Tracks, Lieutenant," he said pointing ahead. "Apaches, maybe five or six warriors passed there since the rain last night."

"Any idea where they are headed?" Franks asked.

"West; probably to the Rio Grande if I was guessing."

"Get on their trail then. Let's see for sure," Franks stated.

~~~

Shakespeare, high on the side of a hill behind a large clump of sage looked at the scene below him and cursed. Below him, sitting on his butt with his hands tied behind him, was the sheriff. Three Apaches were fixing to do some pretty bad things to him Shakespeare figured. 'Three ta wun ain't veree gud odds.' he thought to himself. He watched while trying to come up with a plan. It appeared the Apaches were arguing as to what to do. "Problee abut which wun gets tha honurs," he muttered under his breath.

He figured the rest of the posse went back home.' I wuld have liked ta heer'd tha talk amungst them befur tha gave up and went back,' he thought to himself. As he watched, one of the braves walked over to the sheriff. ' I ain't gonna let him kill him,' he thought as he sighted the sharps in the middle of the braves back. He would shoot if the brave went for his knife or tomahawk.   The brave standing in front of the sheriff suddenly and viciously kicked him in the ribs knocking the sitting sheriff on his back.   He rolled over on his side and pulled his legs up in a fetal position with probably a broke rib or two.

Shakespeare was no more than forty yards away but sometimes shooting at something below you can be tricky, even for an expert shot like him.   He lay his pistol within easy reach, took a cartridge for his sharps and lay it on a rock close to his hand. He figured he could get one easy, if lucky he might get two...the third was doubtful and that's where the rub came in. He figured the third one would kill the sheriff immediately, and his risking his neck to save someone who was trying to kill him, would be wasted.   He wondered why he was doing this anyway...trying to save a man who was tracking him.   He just couldn't let a white man be tortured like he knew the sheriff was gonna be, not if he could help it.

The brave that kicked the sheriff walked back to the others and sat down beside the fire they had going. The other two sat down beside him.   The fire was not a good sign for things to come for the sheriff. Shakespeare let the hammer down carefully on the sharps and relaxed, waiting for things to play out.

~~~

Tye finished his smoke while Delacruz waited patiently for him to suggest something. "If the Apaches are there, maybe we can turn it to our advantage," Tye said suddenly.

"Our advantage!" Delacruz said. "How in hell's bells do we do that?"

"If I know Apaches," Tye said.   "They will have enough men in the rocks on both sides of the canyon to pin us down. When we are pinned down, the main group will charge up the canyon behind us to try and overrun us."

"And your plan?"

"Go in and fall into their trap and then turn it against them."

"RIDE INTO A DAMN TRAP!! Delacruz screamed. "That's not too damn smart, Tye."

Tye held up his hand, "Let me finish, Captain. We will send six men around to the right and have them work their way to the top, looking down on the canyon where we will be riding. They should have the Apaches that are on that side of the canyon with their backs to them, making them easy targets. We will ride into the canyon but leave fifteen men here. The men on top will open up before the Apaches do... hopefully anyway. The gunfire will make the main body of Apaches think we are pinned down and they will come a running. When they are in the canyon, the fifteen men here will charge in behind them. They will be caught between the men coming and us--crossfire. It will work with a little luck."

"What luck are you talking about?"

"Well, I'm guessing the main body of Apaches is to the left of the canyon entrance, hidden in those ravines over there," Tye said pointing. "If they are, the sharpshooters we send to the right will be okay. That's where the luck comes in. The whole plan revolves around the men getting above the Apaches and able to open up on them before they do us."

Delacruz looked hard into Tye's eyes, thinking of the plan and the positives and negatives. It was against a cavalryman's way of thinking to deliberately walk into a trap like that but what Tye said may be true. If so, this whole thing could be over pretty quick.

He turned in the saddle and shouted, "Officers

and non coms, over there," he said, pointing to a clump of mesquite. When they were gathered, Tye knelt in front of them and smoothed out a place on the ground. With a stick he drew a map showing where they were now, the canyon, and where he figured the Apaches to be. He explained his plan, putting emphasis that it all depended on the men getting in position on top.

"Lieutenant Garrison, you will remain here with fifteen men and hide in that large clump of mesquite over there," Delacruz said, nodding toward the mesquites.

"Lieutenant Gorman, I know you are an excellent shot, so you pick six men you know to be good and work your way up to where Tye said you need to be."

"Gorman," Tye said. "We are dead men if you don't get there and shoot first."

"We'll be there, Tye. Count on it," Gorman said.

"We're betting our lives on it, Lieutenant," Tye said, shaking Gorman's hand.

"Pick your men Lieutenant and move out," Delacruz ordered.

"Yes Sir, Captain," he replied, and turned to start picking the best shots to go with him.

"Captain," Tye called. "I think in a case like this, it might be well for all the men to know what's going on; don't you?"

"Sergeant Anderson." Delacruz hollered.

"Yes Sir, Captain, I'm here."

"Assemble the men. We are going to have a pow wow." He smiled at the words 'pow wow'. He didn't know where that expression came from.

The men were aghast at first when they heard the plan and a lot of cuss words went around. It got quiet when Delacruz held up his hand. When they listened to the whole plan, they saw how it might work and most changed their minds. Riding into a trap still didn't set with some. It didn't sit well with Tye either. Gorman and his sharpshooters left and the rest of the men made it look like it was another rest stop. They wanted to give them at least thirty minutes to get into position before starting out. Tye held his breath, waiting for the shots if the main group of Apaches were on the right instead of the left. Gorman had backtracked the way they had come before cutting toward the canyon. It wouldn't work if the Apaches saw them heading for the rim. Garrison and his men went into the mesquites one or two at a time so as not to draw attention.

~~~

Grey Owl, looking thru the glasses that see far, saw Gorman leave and wondered why they had left going back where they come from. It didn't matter, Watkins was still there. That was all that mattered to him. The death of the others was just a bonus. He never, as no Apaches ever did, figure out why the bluecoats had to stop so often. He looked the troops over and then laid the glasses down. He then did the one thing that Apaches did best, wait...wait for the opportunity he dreamed of.

~~~

Back at the fort, Jim was behind the bar wiping shot glasses when he saw Thurston walk in.

"Howdy, Major," he said in his usual jovial voice. "Surprised to see you; what brings you to town?"

"Can't a man just get a beer without being harassed by nosey barkeeps?" Thurston said, laughing and shaking Jim's hand.

96

"Won't ask another question, Major," Jim said throwing his hands up. "Beer?"

"Yeah. Coldest you have." Thurston took the beer and sat down at a table. He was the only one in the saloon besides Jim.

"Business is booming I see."

"Wrong time of the day, Major. Wait about two hours."

Thurston took a long sip, and when Jim looked his way, said... "Come on over and let me buy you a beer, Jim." Jim came over with a beer in his hand and sat down.

"I do have a purpose in coming in to see you," Thurston said.

"Figured you did. What can I do for you, Major?"

Thurston leaned back in his chair. "You know James Taggart, I suppose."Know'um. Can't say I think much of him though."

"Tye and myself think that he's the cause of most of the Indian trouble around here. You heard anything about him?"

"Can't say I have, Major. What do you think he is doing?"

"The cattle the government is sending are not all getting to the Apaches. We think he is keeping most of them and selling them."

"I wonder," said Jim rubbing his chin.

"Wonder what?" Thurston asked.

"There's a cowboy been coming in that just quit a cattle ranch northeast of here. Said there was stuff going on he didn't like. Never thought too much about it till now and didn't ask what stuff he was talking about that was going on."

Thurston leaned forward before speaking. "Who is this man, Jim?"

"Don't know his name but he'll probably be in tonight. He's sweet on one of the girls here."

"Don't suppose you know the name of the rancher he worked for do you?"

"Man by the name of Meechum," Jim answered. "Bill is the name I think." He scratched his jaw for a second, thinking. "Yeah, that's it. Bill Meechum."

"If I come back tonight, can you point him out to me if he's here?"

"Sure, Major. Anything I can do to help."

Thurston finished his beer and left the saloon. Just as he crossed the bridge he ran into O'Malley.

"Sergeant, can you come to my office after dinner tonight? I'd like you to accompany me to Jim's place in Brackett."

O'Malley looked at him sorta funny. "You want me to go with you to a saloon?"

Thurston laughed, realizing how what he said sounded. "I may have a lead on how that scoundrel Taggart is screwing the government. There may be a man there tonight that can answer some of the questions. "

"See you about eight then, Major."

Chapter VIII

Shakespeare watched one of the braves go over to the sheriff and knock him over on his back with his foot. One of the other braves had what looked like wooden stakes and rawhide strips in his hands. They spread eagled the man on the ground and drove the stakes in the ground with a heavy rock and then tied the man's hands and feet to them with the rawhide strips. The third had a bowl shaped piece of mesquite bark and scooped up some of the glowing coals. Shakespeare could see the fear in the sheriff's eyes and even the sweat rolling off his forehead. "Time," Shakespeare muttered and sighted the sharps in the middle of the brave's back that had the coals. He squeezed the trigger and the bullet from the sharps plowed into the man's back, knocking him several feet forward, almost on top of the sheriff. Before the Indian hit the ground, Shakespeare had the pistol leveled at a second brave and pulled the trigger. The bullet plowed into the man's chest, knocking him backwards off his feet. The third grabbed his rifle and was now behind some boulders and sage, eyes searching the canyon walls trying to find the shooter. Shakespeare could not believe that the Apache had not gone ahead and shot the sheriff.

Crawling on his belly, Shakespeare moved away from where he had been and was going to try and get to a position where he would have a shot. He was moving slow not only to be quite but not wanting to raise any dust that could be spotted and his location given away. He had moved about fifty feet when he stopped and chanced a look thru some sage. He could see the sheriff but no Apache where Shakespeare thought him to be. 'He's muving like me.' Shakespeare thought, as he dropped back down on his belly and began crawling again; alert for any sound... anything that might give the Apaches' location away.

He felt good...the excitement...the danger. He hadn't felt this way for a long time. Memories of his days of playing cat and mouse with the Blackfoot in the mountains a long time ago came drifting back to him. God, how he missed those times; he would sell his soul to go back in time to the 'shining times' with him, Ben, and Jim chasing the beaver and those wonderful times at the once a year rendezvous of all the mountain men. He shook his head trying to clear it of those memories. "Best git thos thoghts out uf yur head quick an bac on tha problum heer."

~~~

Tye checked his watch. Thirty minutes had passed since Gorman and the sharpshooters had left. No gunfire had come so far, so he figured he had guessed correctly in that the Apaches would be to the left.

"You ready, Captain?"

"You really think this plan of yours is going to work?" Delacruz questioned.

"Has a good chance if things go our way," Tye replied, looking at Delacruz and smiling.

Delacruz wondered how in hell a man could smile right now, knowing in a few minutes he would be riding into an Apache ambush. 'Hell, I can't even spit,' he thought to himself. He turned in the saddle and gave the command, "by the twos... YO."

The men started out at a walk then picked up the pace to a canter as they approached the canyon. At the mouth of the canyon they would slow to a walk. Tye had given specific instructions for the men to take their feet out of the stirrups as they entered the canyon and to get off their mount as fast as possible with the first shot. No reason for a man getting dragged because he's hung up in them.

As the column entered the canyon they slowed even more. Every man was alert and ready for the first sign of trouble; every eye nervously searching the canyon walls. Tye and the scouts were about twenty yards in front. There was no breeze in the canyon and it was hot, damn hot for this time of the year. 'Guess it could be the situation making it seem this hot,' Tye thought. His eyes, as were the other scouts, were sweeping the canyon walls for any sign of an Apache. They didn't see any, which was no surprise to Tye or them as the Apache was a master at being invisible till he wanted to be seen.

A glint of sunlight got Tye's attention from high on the crest of the canyon. He figured it was Gorman. They were well into the canyon now, almost half way. 'Dammitt,' he thought. 'What in hell is Gorman waiting on?

Gorman and his men had reached the crest and were looking down on the backs of several Apaches that were hidden in the rocks a short distance ahead of where Tye and the scouts were. He saw only two on the far side but knew there was more. He had his men sight in on the Apaches on this side.

"FIRE," he commanded and they fired almost as one and then all hell broke loose. The Apaches that were not killed on this side were firing at him and his men. The Apaches on the other side were firing on the troopers and scouts in the canyon.

Tye had hit the ground with the first shot and scrambled behind a rock. He looked back to see one of the scouts, Goodwill, sprawled on the ground, obviously dead. Billy was crawling to some rocks and had been hit, but Tye couldn't tell where. Dan, the fourth scout was crouched behind some rocks, well protected from the bullets that were splattering rock fragments everywhere. It was almost a comical scene when he looked past his scouts to where the troopers were. He would have laughed any other time but this wasn't the time. Calvary horses were trained to ignore certain things like gunfire but in this canyon, with the shots being echoed off canyon walls, the Apache screams, troopers hollering, and hooves striking rocks, it was exceptionally loud. Horses were rearing up, spinning, and bucking as the men tried to get off. Most did, but as he watched, two were knocked out of the saddle by Apache bullets.

Delacruz was getting his men organized and were firing back at the Apaches in the rocks. As planned, the rest were watching the rear, expecting a charge from the main body any second. Tye had his rifle and one Apache exposed himself for a second too long and Tye sent him to the happy hunting grounds with a shot that exploded the braves head like a ripe watermelon. Some of the men were being injured, not by bullets, but by flying rocks caused by the bullets striking them. The edges were sharp and cut like a knife.

"HERE THEY COME," cried an excited trooper from behind Tye. Tye turned to look and saw the Apaches charging. No matter how many times he saw a charge from them, he was always enthralled by it.; screaming at the top of their lungs, firing their rifles or shooting their arrows, while holding on to their pony with their legs. An Apache could ride his horse like few white men could. The sound of that many more hooves pounding the rocky ground made a deafening sound in the narrow confines of the canyon. They had to be some of the best horsemen in the world. He fired his rifle and saw the lead warrior flip backwards off his racing pony. Tye didn't know if it was his shot or one of the many from the troopers. The Apache charge slowed as they realized the troopers were waiting on them.

An instant later, Garrison charged in behind them with his men in a skirmish line riding at a gallop and the bugler blowing the 'charge' notes. The Apaches, quickly realizing they were trapped, quickened their charge into the canyon intending to ride over the troopers on the ground to escape out the other end. It was close in fighting now, no rifles, only pistols, and in some instances, hand to hand with knives. It was a scene Tye had seen and heard before. The thud of bullets striking flesh, the sickening sound of a tomahawk cracking a skull, screaming of injured and dying men, the thrashing and whinnying of injured horses, and the cursing of struggling men, was an all too familiar sound to him.

Delacruz killed his second Apache with the last shot in his revolver. He had his saber out and as an Apache rode by, swung it in a deadly arc. The Apache saw it coming and tried to avoid it but was too late; his arm was almost severed just above the elbow and he fell hard off his racing pony. Before he could get up, Delacruz struck him again across the neck almost severing the brave's neck.

Tye was aiming his pistol at an Apache, when the extra sense that men like him had, told him there was danger behind him. He whirled about just as one of the Apaches that had been in the rocks was in midair coming down on him. There was no time to fire his pistol. He jumped to the side and the Apache's wild swing with his knife cut into the flesh of his left shoulder. It was only a scratch but the sweat made it burn like hell. The Apache hit the ground hard, stunning him. The couple seconds it took for him to get his senses back proved fatal as Tye was on him with his own Bowie and plunged it deep into the brave's chest, pulled it out and plunged it in again. The braves thrashing stopped. Tye stood up and a soldier next to him was hit in the side of the head by a bullet. He never felt it and was dead before he crashed into Tye.

Grey Owl was livid. His shot was aimed at Tye's head but the soldier appeared from nowhere just as he squeezed the trigger and took the bullet that was meant for Watkins. He could not find the scout again as the smoke was too dense. He was past the last of the troopers and was racing his pony toward the far end of the canyon along with several of his braves. Two were knocked off their ponies by troopers firing from the canyon rim.

Grey Owl knew he had been outsmarted by the scout. The trap he had carefully planned ended up being a trap for them. He had more respect for the bluecoats than before. These men were fighters, like Apaches. He would lick his wounds today, but there would be another day. He headed southwest, not west toward Mexico. He and his men were madder than hell and they were going to find someone to take their frustration out on. It wasn't over.

The Apaches, like only they could, disappeared like smoke in a wind. It was suddenly quiet with only the wounded, both man and animal, making any noise.

As the smoke slowly cleared, Delacruz was appalled by what he saw. Everywhere he looked, men were dead or dying, horses were dead while others were struggling to get on their feet. He had a slight wound in the left arm and a cut on his cheek, probably from a piece of flying rock. He walked slowly, arms hanging loosely with the pistol held loosely in his left hand, his bloody saber in his right. He was in a state of shock, and could not focus on what to do. Suddenly, he felt a strong grip on his shoulder and turned to see Tye. Tye had a canteen and poured it on the captain's bare head. The cool water running down his face and neck brought him to his senses. Tye handed him his hat and patted him on the shoulder.

"We hurt them pretty good, Captain," Tye said.

"Ho...How ma....How many of my men were killed?" Delacruz stammered out.

"Don't know yet, Captain. Sergeant Anderson is getting a count. I would say we gave them a pretty good butt kicking though." He and Delacruz were walking among the wounded when Tye's heart skipped a beat. He saw Billy laying with his head in a sobbing Dan's lap. They were brothers and exceptionally close. Tye had known them for a long time. He knew Billy's wife and each of their two kids. The hole in Billy's stomach made Tye's stomach turn as he knelt down to look at his friend. He knew there was no hope for him, not with the wound where it was. Dan looked at Tye for help, but saw none in Tye's eyes.

Billy opened his eyes and looked at his friend and his brother. One could see the pain in his eyes and face. He knew he was a dead man and was glad his brother and his friend were with him. He was speaking in a low voice and Dan leaned down close to his mouth so he could hear.

"Brother," he whispered, "take care of Consuelo

and my son and daughter for me. Tell them my last thoughts were of them and how much I love them. Sw...Swear to me you will take care of them." Dan looked at Tye. Tye nodded.

"I swear Billy. Tye done told me he would, also. I swear to you they won't need anything..." He stopped when Billy gasped once, and relaxed in his arms. Tears rolled down Dan's face and he hugged Billy's limp body and sat there, rocking back and forth. Tye stood up and turned away from the gut wrenching scene before he broke down, too.

Sergeant Anderson came with the casualty report. Tye stood by Delacruz while Anderson read the report.

"Five dead, thirteen wounded, Sir. Of the wounded, all but three can ride. The enemy had eighteen dead, three captured that were wounded. One of them won't make it. Don't know how many that escaped were wounded."

"I guarantee a lot of them are hit," Tye added.

"Five dead! My God," Delacruz said, shaking his head. Tye knew this was the first time men under the captain's command had been killed. He knew from experience how he felt...what he was thinking.

"Let's take a short walk, Captain," he said putting his hand on Delacruz's shoulder. "I know losing men is a shock, Captain," he said as they walked. "It comes with the territory though. You couldn't expect to never lose a man could you?"

Delacruz shook his head. "No. I knew it would happen sooner or later."

"You did fine Captain. I saw you a couple of times during the fight. You did fine, Sir."

"I appreciate you saying that. Means a lot to me coming from you. But, to be honest, the whole damn mess is fuzzy...like a dream that you can't remember.

107

Is that crazy or what?"

Tye took a few more steps before speaking. "No, not crazy. Sometimes, even when you plan everything to the last detail, things just go to hell when the fighting starts. Things never go as planned...not exactly anyway. You do the best you can but casualties are part of the picture. Learn from what happened and go on. I know the men respected you before and they will even more now. You are a damn good officer and they know it...I know it."

Delacruz looked at Tye and shook his hand. "Thanks, Tye. I'm okay...now." Delacruz turned and began shouting orders. His actions during the fight were noticed by the men and Tye could tell by the reaction of them that they knew they had a leader and that he was in total control. There was no hesitation in following his orders. Lieutenant Gorman, who had come down from the top of the canyon, would lead a small detail that would take the wounded back to the base camp for medical attention. Travois were made for the three that could not ride and good directions were given to Gorman by Tye for getting back. The detail was on its way back to the camp with the dead and wounded within a few minutes.

Delacruz came back to where Tye was and noticed blood on Tye's trousers and shirt.

"Yours or Apache's?" He asked.

"Mine, but it's not serious," Tye said.

"I'll decide that. Let me look at it. Now, get that shirt off."

When the shirt was removed Delacruz was astonished at what he saw, as were some of the troopers that had gathered around. Not so much by the muscular build of the scout, but at the scars over his torso. Tye noticed them staring.

"Pretty ain't they. Got a story with every one,

too," he said smiling.

"You haven't got room for many more," Delacruz said. "But you're right; this wound is the least of the bunch." He cleaned it the best he could, then poured some whiskey on it causing some cursing and dancing around from Tye, resulting in a lot of laughter among the troops. They needed it after the last few minutes of hell they had gone through.

When the stinging from the alcohol ran its course, Tye suggested they find a place to rest up for the night and continue the chase in the morning.

"I know a place not far from here, Captain. It has a spring that always has good water. Might be a good idea to go there for the night and let the men clean up some and get some rest. We can get after Grey Owl early in the morning."

Delacruz agreed and they were soon riding towards the spring. It was near dark when they arrived and camp was set up as soon as the men took care of their mounts. Meals were eaten; sentries put out, and with everyone being exhausted, settled in for the night.

~~~

It was nearing dark and Shakespeare hadn't moved in the last twenty minutes. He had saw the Apache for an instant, moving parallel to him about forty feet below him. Shakespeare had stopped and picked a spot about twenty feet in front of the path he figured the Apache was going where he would be exposed for a couple seconds. Apparently the Apache had stopped also or he would have already crossed the opening that Shakespeare had his sharps trained on. It would be too dark for accurate shooting in a few minutes but he continued to wait, watching, ready for that one second that could mean life or death for himself and the sheriff. He learned a long time ago that in situations like this, patience usually paid off. The man who moved first may not move again...ever.

As he watched he saw a hand reach out and then another as the Apache slowly pulled himself along the ground. He saw the fingers dig into the dirt as the Apache pulled himself into view of his rifle. The Apache's head was in the vee of Shakespeare's sight and the Sharps bucked hard against his shoulder as he fired. The smoke from the sharps prevented him from seeing his bullet enter the Apache's head just above the ear and explode out the other side. When the smoke cleared he saw the unmoving body of the Apache and stood up slowly and painfully, his old joints stiff from lying in one position so long.

"Damn, its tuff gettin old," he muttered to himself as he started down the slope to the sheriff. He saw the look of surprise on the sheriff's face when he recognized who his savior was.

"YOU," he exclaimed. "What in hell are you doing here?"

"Savin' yur sorry ass fur wun thang," Shakespeare said as he cut the rawhide ropes holding his hands and feet to the stakes and looking at the other two dead Apaches. "Luks like thar won't be no partee tonite."

The sheriff, rubbing his bloody wrist where the rawhide had dug into the skin, looked up at Shakespeare.

"Why?"

"Why whut?" Shakespeare asked.

"Why did you come back? You could have been long gone."

"Ain't nev'r left no man ta go thru what yu was fixin' ta go thru. I wus holed up and fixin ta leeve when I hurd ya and them shuting at eech uther. I started toward Fort Clark figurin yu wus going ta get whut yu dezerved but I stopped,   tho't abut it and jus kuldn't du it.   I kuld not leeve no white man ta be killed if'n I kuld help it, not even wun tha wus wantin ta kill me."

Rafferty stood up and looked down at the small, frail looking old man that had just saved his life. "Whatever the reason, I'm glad you did." He reached out his hand which Shakespeare accepted with his own. "It's hard for a man to admit when he was wrong... but I was.   I knew that my brother would end up being killed over his cheating.   I tried to get him to quit but it was like he never heard me.   Blood is thick you know. I hope you will accept my apology for putting you through all this and especially, my thanks for saving my life."

"Let's git outa here." Shakespeare said. "Thar's a kave bout a mile up tha trail. We can spen tha nite thar and I can luk at those wunds uf yurs." It was full dark when they scrambled up the hill to the cave.

Chapter IX

The patrol from Fort Inge, led by Lieutenant Franks, was making camp at the same time at another spring about fifteen miles southwest of the spring where Tye and the column from Clark were camped. Lieutenant James Rogers was in charge of setting up the sentry schedule which he was doing with Sergeant Baker. After completing his task, he sat by the small fire and watched the sun setting behind the low hills. He was beat and he suddenly realized he was starving. He reached into his saddle bags and brought out some jerky and biscuit. He cut off a small, green mesquite limb and poked it thru the biscuit. Holding the biscuit above the flames to get it hot, he chewed some jerky and watched the sunset. It was beautiful with a hundred shades of color filtering around and thru the clouds. He studied the hills thru the darkening shadows and for the first time realized just how wild and actually beautiful this country was. 'Never thought I'd think that,' he thought to himself. So far, everything had been fine. The living conditions were not what he was used to and the food was a little sparse, but he was adapting quite well. He had been inquisitive of his fellow officers and the scout, Wilson. He had even visited with, to some of their surprise, the enlisted men and they had responded to him. Every day, every hour, he thanked Tye for the advice he had given him on the coach.

From the crest of a nearby hill, a pair eyes was watching him and the men as they set up camp. Grey Owl smiled at the thought of killing all the bluecoats, especially the one with the yellow hair. His golden scalp would look impressive on his lance with the other scalps. It would deserve a special place on his lance; next to Watkins's scalp. He backed down from the crest of the hill carefully, not wanting to dislodge any rocks that would alert the bluecoats to his presence. When at the bottom, he mounted his pony and walked a short distance before galloping to his camp, about a mile away. He thought the Great Spirit was giving him another chance to save face after the disaster earlier today with the bluecoats led by Watkins. 'These men have no Watkins,' he said to himself. He figured the bluecoats would continue their same path when the sun came up that they had been traveling this day. He would have a surprise waiting for them along their path.

~~~

It was eight O'clock back at the fort when Thurston and O'Malley entered Jim's saloon and took a table close to the back wall. Jim brought each of them a beer.

"That's the man you want to talk to over there at the bar with the blue shirt, Major," Jim said nodding his head toward the bar.

"Would you ask him to join us?" Thurston asked. Jim nodded and walked over to the man and said something in his ear and the man looked at Thurston and nodded his head. He picked up his beer and slowly walked over to their table and stood there.

"You want to see me?" He asked.

Thurston stood up, reached across the table to

shake the man's hand.   My name is Thurston, and this is Sergeant Major O'Malley."   The man took Thurston's hand.

"Names Dobbs.   Robert Dobbs." He nodded his head in recognition of O'Malley.

"Please have a seat Mr. Dobbs," Thurston said.

"What's this all about?" Dobbs asked.   He had a gut feeling he knew and was nervous as hell, figuring he was in trouble. "Am I in trouble with the Army?"

"I hope not Mr. Dobbs, but I think you can help us out by answering a few questions."

"How's that?" Dobbs said.   It was obvious to both Thurston and O'Malley he was nervous as hell. Dobbs drank the last of his beer.

"Jim," Thurston shouted. "Bring us another round when you can.   Now, Mr. Dobbs, it has come to our attention that you recently worked on a ranch owned by Bill Meechum." Dobbs nodded his head.

"Exactly what kind of work did you do for him?"

"What the hell kind of work do you think I did? I'm a ranch hand and that's a ranch." Dobbs said, visibly upset at such a stupid question.

"Why did you quit?   There can't be much work around here for ranch hands; mostly goats and sheep hereabouts."

Jim brought the drinks and Dobbs took a long drink before setting the mug down and wiping his mouth with his sleeve. "Only reason I stayed was because of that.   Myself, Joe Gurney, Larry Johnson, and Billy Williams, knew something was fishy about the ranch but like you said, they ain't many jobs around here and we wasn't involved in nothing.   Just working the ranch.   I finally had enough and pulled stakes.   I figure the others will soon enough."

Nothing was said for a moment, then Thurston spoke. "What do you mean by 'fishy'?" Thurston asked.

"About once a month these men from San Antonio would bring twenty or thirty cattle. We would meet them and take most of them to the ranch. Five or six would be given to the man from Brackett."

"What's this man's name, the one from Brackett?" Thurston asked now, believing he was fixing to get the goods on that bastard, Taggart.

"Can't say as I ever heard. He would sign some papers and give it to the men from San Antonio and we wouldn't see him again till the next month."

"Could you tell me what this man looked like?"

"Wasn't much to look at. He was a small man, always wore dark suit and string tie. Now the man with him, that's different."

"What do you mean, different?"

"Biggest, ugliest man I ever saw. Musta weighed two hundred and fifty pounds or more, and he wasn't fat. Had small pig eyes, fat lips and a head that seemed too small for that body. One character none of us wanted to mess with."

That was enough to convince Thurston that Taggart was the little man in this story.

"Let me ask you one more question, Mr. Dobbs," Thurston said. "Can you lead me to this Meechum's ranch?"

"Guess so, but can you tell me exactly what's going on?"

O'Malley spoke up. "The bastard is taking most of the cattle for himself that was intended for the Apaches. The Apaches are starving and that's the cause of most of the unrest and anger."

"Me and the boys figured something like that. We're honest cowhands, Major. We ain't no damn thieves. If I lead you out there, what about my friends?"

Thurston thought for a minute. "Tell you what

Dobbs. You lead us there and I'll let you tell the men what's going on and that we are on to them. If they get out, then I promise you nothing will happen to them. If they stay, then they will suffer the consequences."

"Fair enough, Major. By the way, Meechum has seven hard cases working for him."
Thurston and O'Malley stood up. "We will leave at first light. I trust you will be there."

"I'll be there, Major. You can count on it." Dobbs stood up and the three shook hands. Dobbs returned to the bar, and O'Malley and Major Thurston left, walking back to the fort. "Get a ten man detail together for in the morning, Sergeant."

"Yes Sir, Major. See you at first light."

~~~

"Column is a hell of lot smaller than when we left Fort Clark," Dan commented.

"Afraid it may get smaller before this is over," Tye answered. They were sitting on their mounts in the shade of a large mesquite, watching the column approach them. It was mid morning and with the low cloud cover it was a lot cooler than expected. It would be a great day under different circumstances. Chasing Apaches would ruin any day, no matter how perfect the weather was. The cool air did feel good for a change, though. Tye figured it would probably rain later in the day.

"Hadn't had much of a chance to tell you how sorry I am about Billy. He was a good friend," Tye said.

Dan put both hands on the pommel of his saddle and stared skyward. "He would have loved this day. He always liked stormy weather and I think today will be one of those days." He looked at Tye. "You was his

116

friend, too. Billy never talked much you know, and he didn't have many friends. He was proud you were one of them." He reached and put his hand on Tye's shoulder. "I'm glad you are my friend." Tye reached and put his hand on Dan's shoulder and both held their hands on each other's shoulders for a few seconds, nodded their heads to acknowledge the moment, then turned their attention to the arriving column.

They had traveled about ten miles since daybreak. Delacruz spoke, "Think it's time for a break, Tye?"

"My sentiments exactly, Captain," Tye answered as he dismounted and loosened the cinch on Sandy's saddle. He took some oats from a saddlebag and put them into his hat and let Sandy munch on them while he scratched him between the ears. When the oats were gone, he poured some water in his hat and offered it which Sandy lapped up quickly. He led Sandy to a patch of shade under an extremely tall mesquite and let him munch on a patch of short grama grass. Each trooper did the same for their mounts.

"Why do you figure the Apaches are heading southwest instead of west toward Mexico?" Delacruz asked.

"My guess is they're mad, Captain. Mad as hell and are probably looking to find someone to take their anger out on. Something else I've been thinking about, Captain. I think it would be a good idea for me to ride and try to get ahead of them and warn any homesteads that are in their path. Dan here can keep you on their trail."

Delacruz scratched the back of his neck, something he always did unconsciously when he was thinking. He didn't like the idea of Tye leaving them but then again, his duty was to save as many lives as possible from the rampaging Apaches.

"Do you think it's a good idea to go alone?" he asked.

Tye laughed. "Captain, I've spent more time alone out here than with the good company of men like you. Besides, I can move faster alone and not have the burden of worrying about anyone else."

Delacruz stood up from the crouched position he had been in and told Tye to go ahead. "When can I expect you back with us?"

Tye thought for a moment. "I'll find you mid morning tomorrow." He turned and tightened the cinch on the saddle, mounted Sandy, and with a wave, he was gone. Delacruz immediately had a feeling he should have sent someone with him, regardless of what Tye said.

.

~~~

Southwest of where Tye was, Lieutenant Franks waited patiently with his patrol about a hundred yards from the canyon opening. He was waiting on his scout to give the all clear sign before he took the patrol in. He had a bad feeling in his gut, regardless of the fact that no sign of any Apaches had been found. He mentioned this to the young Lieutenant Rogers who was sitting astride his mount beside him.

"One of the things Tye told me was that an experienced man should always go with gut feelings out here," Rogers said..."A man like yourself. He also said that when you don't see any sign of Apaches, look out." Nothing else was said for a few minutes. Then Rogers commented.

"We could go around and bypass this canyon."

"I know we could, but it would throw us at least a half day behind. I know this area and it would take us fifteen miles out of the way." Franks took the makings out and rolled a miserable excuse for a smoke. Rogers saw Frank's hand trembling and looked away not wanting the Lieutenant to notice he saw it.

Franks just inhaled the first puff when the all clear signal was given by the scout. He turned in his saddle and told Sergeant Baker to pass the word for the men to get their rifles out and be ready. "BY THE TWO'S...YO," his raised arm dropped, and the patrol started out. Rogers looked back at the fifteen men, mostly seasoned veterans, and saw they were ready. He took his pistol out and checked the load and placed it loosely back in its holster, flap unsnapped.

They entered the canyon at a trot. The floor was relative free of obstacles and the far end, about a quarter mile away, could be seen by all. The pace picked up to a canter as Franks wanted to get thru as fast as possible. They were half way thru when he threw up his hand to halt the column. Suddenly, out of nowhere at the far end of the canyon was a dozen warriors. Looking back, they saw a dozen more behind them.

"SHIT! Franks exclaimed loudly. "INTO THE ROCKS ALONG THE CANYON WALL!" He shouted. They made an unorganized charge to get to the protection of the boulders. When they were about forty yards from the shelter of the boulders, a volley came blasting at them from the rocks. Franks did a cartwheel off the back of his mount, shot square thru the brisket and dead before he hit the rocky ground. Five other men, including the scout, were blasted out of their saddles and two were hanging on, wounded.

"FOLLOW ME! Rogers hollered above the noise of the rifles. He swerved to the right and hit the rocks about a hundred yards to the right of where the Apaches were that had been hidden in the rocks. He was off his mount before it completely stopped, turned and saw the remaining men were with him and flying off their mounts.

"GET YOUR CANTEENS AND EXTRA AMMO POUCHES! Rogers shouted. Some of the men did, others didn't as they were simply wanting to get buried in the rocks away from the Apache rifles. Just as they settled in, the Apaches that were in front of them were charging, screaming and firing their rifles. 'MY GOD.' Rogers thought, this is what Tye was talking about. The hair was standing at attention on the back of his neck, but surprisingly, he was in control.   "FIRE!" He commanded and a deadly volley knocked four Apaches off their ponies and had one more draped over his pony. The charge broke and the men let out a cheer.

Rogers took a second to look around where he had led the men.   He was surprised it was as good as it was.   "Sergeant Baker!" He hollered.

"Yes Sir." came the reply to his right, from behind some rocks.

"Get a man in position behind us to keep the Apaches from filtering thru the rocks and surprising us."

"Yes sir, right away, Sir."

"Jesse," he bellowed.   "Get back in the rocks and watch our backs."

"Yo!" came the reply from back in the rocks.

The Apaches that were behind them, had arrived and joined the others. There were about eighteen or twenty now in front of them. He had no idea how many were still in the rocks.   They were outnumbered at least two, maybe three or four to one. His mind was racing as he surveyed the terrain.   The Apaches could only come from two ways, a frontal assault or from the rocks.   He figured he had about eight, maybe nine men, counting the wounded. He needed someone to get advice from but the scout had been one of the first to go down, along with Franks.

A rifle shot followed by two quick pistol shots startled everyone.

"JESSE, YOU OKAY?" Shouted Sergeant Baker.

"Yo," came a reply from the rocks. "Knocked two down, Sergeant. Rest retreated back into the rocks."

"Good job, Jesse," Baker hollered back. "You stay sharp. I'll have someone relieve you in awhile."

"Yo," came the reply from Jesse.

The Apaches on horseback had retreated a safe distance away. Rogers relaxed some, and then realized how dry his mouth was. He took a small swallow from is canteen, savored it for a moment, then swallowed, replacing the cap.

"Go easy on the water men," he shouted. He suddenly heard rocks rattling to his right, jerked his head around to see Sergeant Baker and the men coming to him.

"Where do you want the men deployed, Lieutenant?" Baker asked. Actually realizing for the first time that he was in command, Rogers hesitated, and then started pointing to different places where the men should take up their defenses.

"Each one of you take a drink, and then give your canteens to Sergeant Baker. You are in charge of the water Sergeant. Make it last." He handed Baker his and each man did the same. Two men didn't have theirs but got a drink from a buddy.

"Partner up men. One watch while the other rests. We may be here awhile till we can sort things out and figure a way out." The men were all deployed within a twenty yard strip of large boulders that one could almost stand fully erect behind and still be well protected. Baker was behind the same boulder as Rogers. One man was still in the rocks behind them and one had the horses behind a boulder as large as a house. Their position was a strong one and Rogers thought they would be okay, but for how long he didn't know. He knew the water and food they had wouldn't last long. He was surprised how relaxed he was...feeling in total control of his emotions. He could feel the men's eyes on him and he knew they were depending on him to get them out of this mess. 'One hell of a situation for a greenhorn like me to be in,' he thought to himself.

"Sergeant, keep a watch. I'm going to scout around and study our position some."

"Yes sir."

"You men okay?" He asked two privates that were behind the first boulder he came to.

"Yes sir," one replied.

"D...Do you think we have a chance, Sir?" The other asked his voice cracking.

"Sure we do. Do you think I want a massacre on my record for my first patrol?" he replied smiling, trying to be positive to them.

He patted one on the shoulder and then continued his exploration of their position speaking with each man and looking at the wounds of two. They were painful, but both could stand and fire their weapons. He reminded each to stay in the protection of the boulders and to keep a sharp watch.

When he arrived back at his position with Sergeant Baker, he was convinced he was lucky in finding the spot he had led them. The only problem was food and water.

"Sit in the shade, Sergeant. I'll watch awhile." His eyes searched every nook and cranny in front of their position. He could see nothing...nothing was moving, not even a bird.

~~~

The gray light of dawn found Shakespeare and Sheriff Rafferty finishing off the last drop of the coffee Shakespeare had made. "Twas me," Shakespeare was saying. "I'd hole up durin tha lite uf day and travul at nite."

"Why do you say that?"

"Thos dead Injuns or gonna have frens uf thars luking fur'm."

Rafferty thought about it for a moment.

"Yeah. You may be right. You heading on to Fort Clark?"

"Yep, but I'm changin my direcshun. Thos Paches tha jumped yu yesterday kame down tha trail frum tha direcshun I   wus headed.

"You gonna hole up with me till dark?"

Shakespeare laughed. "Nope. Said tha a minute ago cause yu're a damn pilgrim when it kumes ta knoing Injuns and you'd problee stumble right into a mess uf 'em."

Any other time big Rafferty would have punched someone that smart mouthed him like that but the events of yesterday had humbled him a little. He realized how close he had been to dying. He just laughed and shook Shakespeare's hand and again told him how grateful he was.

"Yu be karefull," Shakespeare said. "Wun more thang sheriff. If'n any Apaches do kume along tha trail, hold yur horse so he wun't whinnee or snort at tha smell or sight uf tha 'pache's ponees. I'll wipe out tha tracs whare we left tha trail and heeded up ta this kave."

He waved at Rafferty when he finished and headed on toward Fort Clark and his long awaited meeting with Ben's son.

THE CROSSING

Chapter X

Major Thurston, O'Malley, Dobbs, and ten troopers were over half way to Meechum's ranch by noon. The ranch was located northwest of Uvalde and Fort Inge. The fort was real close to Uvalde like Fort Clark was to Brackett. They had been alternately walking and trotting their horses and were making good time.

"Time for a break," Thurston told O'Malley as he raised his arm and signaled for the men to halt.

O'Malley turned in his saddle. "Twenty minutes. Take care of your mounts first." O'Malley had to hide his smile watching Thurston get off his horse and walking to a large flat rock, and gingerly sitting down. Thurston hadn't been on a horse very much for the last six months and the soft chair in his office hadn't done much to keep his butt in condition to sit a saddle. Thurston caught O'Malley smiling and had to laugh himself.

"Remind me to not go this long again without being in the saddle." Dobbs came over to them.

"How much farther to the ranch, Dobbs?"

Dobbs looked to the northwest and scratched his chin for a moment.

"About fifteen miles or so. Should be there before nightfall, I'd say."

"Good, now get some of this delicious army food in your belly." He laughed and tossed Dobbs some jerky and a hard biscuit.

"Hell, ya'll don't eat no better'n us cowhands when we're on the range," he said laughing.

Nothing else was said and they all enjoyed the 'great food'. The brief rest was good for them though.

~~~

Tye had heard shots farther to the southwest and was headed toward them. He figured the Apaches had attacked a homestead but wasn't sure because of the number of shots that was fired. "Sounds like a damn war, Sandy," he said as he galloped in the direction of the gunfire. He figured it was about a mile away. He would have never heard them if the breeze hadn't been blowing from that direction.

He stopped and dismounted when he thought he was close. Carefully, he made his way up a steep hill. At the top, he removed his hat and peered around a clump of yucca. He was looking down at the Apaches who were about three hundred yards up the canyon. Looking directly below him, he saw the troopers.

"Damn. If they aren't in a hell of a mess, I ain't ever saw one." He quickly took in the situation and the terrain. He spotted the soldier back in the rocks. 'Good move there,' he thought to himself. He spotted a way he thought he could make his way down without being seen. He watched as the troopers prepared to defend themselves as the Apaches were coming again. The Apaches were screaming their insults as their horses' hooves pounded the rocky floor of the canyon. Tye took advantage of the noise and began climbing down to the soldiers.

Lieutenant Rogers, momentarily enthralled by

the sight, shouted, "Have your pistols out and use them after you fire your rifle. Don't try to reload your rifle. WAIT TILL I SAY FIRE," he screamed over the noise of the pounding hooves and screaming Apaches.

The Apaches were getting close now and the ground was starting to shake with the pounding of their ponies. At fifty yards, Rogers gave the order. "FIRE!" As one, the troopers fired and more Apaches left their ponies. The Apaches were firing from their racing ponies and one of the troopers was hit, but not seriously. The men used their pistols at twenty-five yards and several more ponies were rider less. The attack broke off, but one trooper was killed and another hit in the shoulder, besides the one hit a moment earlier. The Apaches had nine braves lying on the ground and a couple barely able to stay on their ponies. It appeared the two were hit pretty hard.

'They won't try that again for awhile,' Tye thought to himself. "Whoever that Lieutenant is, he's pretty cool." He started working his way closer, moving carefully from rock to rock, so as not to draw attention. He got within about ten yards of the troopers and decided he had better make his presence known so he wouldn't get shot by a nervous trooper.

"You men in the rocks. Don't shoot. I'm coming in."

"WHAT THE HELL?" Baker shouted.

"Hold your fire," Rogers ordered. "Come on in."

Tye stood up and walked toward them.

"I'll be dammed," Rogers shouted and surprised the men by moving quickly toward this stranger.

"Lieutenant Rogers," Tye was as surprised as Rogers was as they shook hands.

"You in command here, Lieutenant?" The scout asked.

"Yes Sir. Lieutenant Franks was, but he was

killed right off."

"You led your men here, to this place then?"

"Yes Sir. Didn't have much of a choice. The Apaches had both ends bottled up and then some more in the rocks opened up on us. That's when Lieutenant Franks and the scout were killed."

Tye looked around. "You did a good job of picking a spot out." The troopers gathered around wondering who in hell this man was that sneaked past the man in the rocks behind them.

"Men," Rogers said, "This is the scout from Fort Clark all of you have heard about, Tye Watkins." A murmur went around the men as they couldn't believe Watkins was here. Their hopes rose immediately and they were all ears when Tye spoke.

"There's no way I can get you and your horses out the way I came," Tye stated bluntly.

"Then how we gonna get out of this fix?" an excited trooper asked.

"I'm leading a patrol of about thirty men. We kicked the hell out of this bunch yesterday and I was trying to get ahead of them to warn the homesteaders when I heard the shooting. Lieutenant Rogers has you in a good defensive position here. I don't think the Apaches will try a frontal assault again. They will try to wait you out. They know you ain't going nowhere and you have a limited amount of water and food. They won't be in no hurry."

"What will we do then?" another asked.

"Let Tye finish," Lieutenant Rogers ordered, holding up his hand.

"I think I can be back here before nightfall with the patrol. You just need to follow Roger's orders till then. He's kept you alive so far." He shook each of their hands and then disappeared like a ghost back into the rocks leaving each man with something they did not have a few minutes before...hope.

"Sergeant Baker, give each man some water
and then each of you get back to your post.
Private Holmes, can you handle a rifle with that
shoulder?"

"Yes Sir, no problem, Sir." He said with new
confidence that reflected in his voice. Each man knew
that maybe this wasn't going to be their last sunset.
Each one of the men had something else also, respect
for this young Lieutenant.

~~~

Grey Owl wasn't pleased with what had
happened so far.   He was learning that these
bluecoats were not at all like the ones at the
homestead a few days ago.   These were brave men...
fighting men, like the one's yesterday. They were
almost like an Apache warrior.   He would not risk
losing more men.   The bluecoats were not going
anywhere and time was on his side. Two men had left
to get fresh meat and water.   They would make camp
and wait.

~~~

It was late afternoon when Thurston and the
patrol arrived at the Meechum ranch. They stopped
behind a hill, about a quarter of a mile from the main
house.

"Dobbs," Thurston said, "You have thirty
minutes to ride in and see if your friends want out or
not." Dobbs nodded and galloped toward the ranch.

"Damn," Thurston said as he dismounted. He
rubbed his butt with both hands. "Never again will I
not get on a horse regularly." He didn't sit, just walked

around looking at his watch.

"Riders coming," the sentry hollered.

"It's Dobbs, with two men." shouted the sentry.

"Only Two? I thought he said there were three," O'Malley said

Dobbs and two riders came around the hill and dismounted. "Major, this here is my friends I was telling you about. This is Joe Gurney and Larry Johnson." Dobbs said as they shook hands with the Major.

"What about the other one? You said there were three," Thurston said.

"Billy Williams is up north about three miles with some cattle and one of Meechum's boys," the one named Gurney said. "He's like us Major, knew something was fishy but didn't know what."

"MOUNT UP", Thurston ordered.

"Wait a minute, major," Dobbs said. "Meechum and the men are gone to town. Left early today said they would be back before dark. Is that right, Gurney?"

Gurney nodded his head.

"All right, we'll wait then," Thurston said. "Sergeant O'Malley, have the men take their mounts and themselves to the shade of that cliff over there," he said pointing toward the place.

"Yes Sir, anything else, Sir."

"Assign a man to watch the ranch for Meechum and his men."

"Yes Sir." Thurston walked to the shade and sat down on a fairly flat rock...gingerly, wincing as he rear touched the rock.

~~~

Tye had been pushing Sandy for about forty five minutes when he spotted the patrol. He passed Dan without a word and headed to the front of the column where Delacruz was.

"Tye, what are you doing back? What's wrong?"

"I found the Apaches, Sir. They have a patrol from Inge bottled up in a canyon yonder." He pointed to the southwest. "The patrol's in a good defensive position but they have been hit pretty hard. Down to about nine men, I'd say. I got to them and told them I'd be back with the patrol."

"How far away are they?" Delacruz questioned.

"Forty five or so minutes."

"Looks like you rode Sandy pretty hard. Can he make it back?"

"He'll make it, Lieutenant. Let's go. If we can get there before it's too late, we can trap the damn Apaches and get this mess over with."

"Lead the way, Tye. We're right behind you," Delacruz said.

THE CROSSING

Chapter XI

The patrol covered the distance in a little more than thirty minutes. Tye held them at the base of a steep hill.

"Keep the men here Captain while I check things out. They should be just over the hill." Tye dismounted and moved up the steep slope. He was at the same spot he was earlier in the day. He looked over and nothing had changed. "Thank God," He mumbled to himself. He worked his way back down the slope to the patrol.

All the men were dismounted and gathered around Tye and Delacruz. Tye picked up a stick, and started drawing marks on the ground. "This is the canyon over that hill I was just on. It runs east and west, our right and left. The Apaches are here," and he marked an X on the ground. "The Inge men are here, and we are here." He put two other X's on the ground, stood up and let Delacruz tell them the plan they had discussed.

"Lieutenant Garrison, you will lead fifteen men along with the scout, August, and form a skirmish line and charge thru from the west end of the canyon. Pistols and sabers only. Rifles are not worth a damn from a running horse, besides, it will be close in fighting.   Tye and myself will take the rest of the men thru the east end of the canyon. With our firepower and yours, along with the men from Inge in the rocks, we should have them trapped," he stood up and held his hand out and closed his fist. "Trapped like a bunch of damn rats. Lieutenant, you have ten minutes to get in position. When you hear our bugler, you will attack."

"Yes Sir."

"Move out," Delacruz ordered. Tye looked at the sun and figured they had about thirty minutes of light left.

"We're cutting it damn close, Sandy," Tye mumbled as he mounted his horse.

.

~~~

It was less than an hour before sunset and Thurston was concerned that the men they were after weren't coming back tonight. A couple minutes later, the sentry shouted at him.

"Riders approaching the ranch, Major."

"How many riders?" There was a moment's pause before the sentry answered.

"Seven, Sir."

"That should be all of them," Dobbs said.

"We'll give then a few minutes, and then ride in," Thurston said. "Get the men mounted, Sergeant. Thurston mounted his horse, wincing when he sat in the saddle. O'Malley noticed how gingerly Thurston had sat in the saddle.

"That ole saddle kinda hard, major?"

"No harder than it ever was but my butt ain't in the same condition it used to be." They both smiled.

"By the two's...Yo." They moved out at a walk. When they were one hundred yards from the ranch house, on a signal from Thurston, they broke right and left forming a skirmish line. "Rifles on the ready," Thurston ordered and each man pulled their rifles from the saddle scabbard, placed the rifle butt on their thighs, barrels pointed skyward.

They halted twenty yards from the house. "Sergeant O'Malley, take two men and stand in front of the bunkhouse in case some are in there."

When O'Malley was in position, he hailed the house.

"You men in the house, come out." There was scuffling of chairs inside. "Who's there?" Came a deep voice from the house.

"Major Thurston, Post Commander out of Fort Clark."

"What the hell do you want with us?"

"I have your house under twenty guns. If that door doesn't open and I see men coming out by the time I count to three, we will open up. ONE, TWO....

"Okay. Okay. Hold your fire. We're coming out." The door opened and five men filed out the door. "There should be seven of you. Where's the others?"

"Here, Sir," O'Malley had the two men that were in the bunkhouse walking in front of him and his men.

The men were herded in front of Thurston and the troopers. Thurston turned to one of his men. "Take their weapons, private. Make damn sure you get all of them, including the knives.

"Now wait just a min..."

"Shut your damn mouth," Thurston ordered.

"Why don't you shut it for me, soldier boy." The private that was disarming the men dropped the weapons and put all one hundred fifty pounds into a vicious right that caught the man flush on the chin. He hit the ground, out cold. Thurston held back a smile.

"Which of you men is Meechum?" Not a word was said. "Sergeant O'Malley, would you assist me please?"

"Yes Sir, Major. Be glad to." O'Malley said as

he dismounted, and walked over to the men standing in front of the Major. "Who's Meechum?" He asked. A tough looking hombre spit some tobacco juice on the ground near O'Malley's boot. O'Malley looked down at the tobacco and the big Irishman hit the man full on the nose with a giant fist that had all two hundred plus pounds behind it. Bones crunched and blood spurted and the man was sprawled on the ground, moaning. O'Malley stepped to the next man.

"Meechum?" He asked. No one said a word.

"I'm gonna enjoy this, Major."

He drew back his fist and the man in front of him threw up his hands in front of his face. "That's Meechum," he said pointing to a short, very stocky, dangerous looking man. His face looked like leather from too much sun. Meechum looked at the man who pointed him out and if looks could kill, the man would be dead.

"Meechum, you and your men are under arrest for stealing government property," Thurston stated matter of factly. "Private, you take two men and go to the corral and saddle seven horses. "O'Malley, take a man and go with Dobbs to get the other two, including Dobb's friend." In a few minutes, the privates returned with the saddled horses. "Get them mounted and then tie their hands behind their backs. Make damn sure they can't get loose." With this done, they started the trip back to Fort Clark. Thurston was dreading it. He could feel ever step his horse took with his sore butt.

~~~

Only a few minutes of daylight was left and Tye knew they had cut it close, real close. He, Delacruz and the men were in position at the mouth of the canyon on the east end. Delacruz checked his watch.

"Okay bugler, cut loose." As the bugler sounded charge, his men broke around the hill and into the canyon. They were in a skirmish line and were at a gallop.

The men in the rocks were up in an instant when they heard the bugler. Never had any heard a prettier sound nor ever saw a prettier sight than the blue uniforms and the flag snapping in the wind.

"Follow me," Lieutenant Rogers ordered. They were out of the rocks and ran a few yards and then he had them kneel and ready with their rifles.

Garrison started his men in the west end of the canyon at the sound of the bugle. The Apaches were trapped. They made a run for the west end of the canyon, intending to run thru the bluecoats and escape the trap. It was another in a long line of mistakes that Grey Owl had made the last two days. The bluecoats pulled up their mounts, dismounted, kneeled and fired a volley from thirty yards knocking almost half of the Apaches off their ponies. The Apaches swerved to the left and a volley from Rogers and his men knocked six more down. Eight Apaches were left making a break for the mouth of the canyon and safety. Tye and four men were kneeling and firing. Three fell off their ponies and flopped like rag dolls when they hit the ground. Five escaped unscathed. Garrison and his men started to chase them but Delacruz had the bugler sound recall.

Garrison and his men rode up to where Delacruz and his men were.

"Looks like you got most of them, Captain."

"We kicked the hell out of them but five or six got away," Delacruz said in a somber tone. "Thought we could end it here but it's not over till ever damn one of them is accounted for." Garrison sat with his hands on his pommel, his weight on his hands taking some of the weight off his butt.

"Where's Tye?" Delacruz nodded toward the men from Inge who were whooping and hollering, waving their hats. Garrison saw Tye walking toward a Lieutenant and shaking his hand.

"God, it's good to see you, Sir," Rogers said shaking Tye's hand. As he did so, the other men came up and did the same. They shook the men's hands that were with Tye as well. It was a joyous moment for the beleaguered men from Inge. They had been jerked from the jaws of certain death by this man and the men from Clark.

No injuries had been sustained by the men from Fort Clark during the action. Now came the gruesome task of retrieving Lieutenant Franks and the others killed earlier. They found the men. Most wish they hadn't. The bodies were butchered beyond belief. Lieutenant Rogers got sick as did some of the other men. Later, after the remains were wrapped tightly in blankets with the ends tied securely to keep the smell down so not to spook the horses, night camp was set up. It was full dark by the time the fires were lit and coffee was boiling. The men's spirits were pretty low after that task, but as always with an army man, the aroma of boiling coffee lifted them up.

Sitting around the fire, Rogers had some questions. "Why do they do that to men after they are dead?"

Tye poked a stick into the fire causing sparks to fly. "Apaches are like other tribes, they believe in life after death. Not exactly the way we believe in the hereafter but they believe a man will go into the hereafter the way he looked at the time of his death. If you cut a man's head off, he will go there with no head. If you cut his hands off, he will have no hands, etc. Don't get the idea that they are vicious savages,

139

Lieutenant. Almost everything you see them do, the white man and the Mexicans have done to them, or worse."

"You told me that they were smart, good fighters and tacticians and hard to fool or trap. Yet, these were easy pickings for you," Rogers said. By now, most of the men from Inge were around the fire, listening.

"Did you notice anything strange about those dead Apaches, Lieutenant?"

"No, but then that's the first ones I ever saw," Rogers answered, bringing a few guffaws from the men. Tye laughed.

"Oh yeah. I forgot you were a fresh, snotty nosed Lieutenant on your first patrol," he said still laughing. Then, when everyone was thru chuckling over the comment Tye added, "They were kids. Just damn kids. The ones I looked at could not have been more than in their late teens. You have a whole different game Lieutenant, when you are dealing with seasoned warriors. In fact, none of you would probably be here now if that was the case. Seasoned warriors would have some men on the hill that I was on as soon as you had taken up positions in those rocks. With them shooting at your backs and the others from the front..." He paused, letting them imagine the scene. "How many of you have had an encounter with the Apaches before today?" One man raised his hand. He was an older, tough looking veteran. Tye figured him to be one who has been promoted and busted several times. "You agree with me about the older warriors?" The man nodded his head. "Make sure that man is on your next patrol, Lieutenant. He can help you out if the going gets tough." The man sat a little straighter, his head held a little higher after the compliment.

One of the Inge men spoke up. "We've heard you been fighting Apaches since you were fourteen years old. Is that right?"

"Pretty much. I was born near here and every once in a while some young bucks would decide to try out pa and me...mostly pa. He was big medicine to them...a great warrior they said and it would be a great honor to kill him in battle."

"From what I hear you have taken your pa's place on their honor roll," the man said.

"That's one damn honor roll I wouldn't want to be on," said another, bringing more laughter.

"Gets to be pretty tiresome sometimes at that," Tye said laughing.

The coffee was ready and everyone at Tye's fire had a cup. They were relaxed, talking and asking questions. One of the tougher ones came from Lt. Rogers. "Why do the Apaches do what they do to men? I mean, why do they torture their prisoners for so long? Why don't they just kill them right off?"

"I asked my pa that same question years ago," Tye answered. "He explained to me that the Apache believe they get the person's strength or power of their enemies they kill. The longer it takes them to die the more of this strength or power comes to them. I believe that is one reason they despise a coward so much because they get no power from killing him." Other questions followed and Tye answered every one with his usual straightforward, honest answers. When it was time to turn in he said he had one more thing to say.

"Two things saved you men's butts today. One was the fact I mentioned earlier about it being young, inexperienced warriors. The second is the action taken by this young Lieutenant." He put his hand on Roger's shoulder. "His quick action after Lieutenant Frank's

141

death had a lot to do with your being here now. I know he has a lot to learn and he'll make some mistakes like we all do, but as my pa used to say about a fighting man, he'll do to ride the river with." With that said, he shook their hands and accepted their thanks again and walked back to his fire. He left several men happy to have seen another sunset, a sunset they hadn't expected to see just a few hours earlier. He also left a young Lieutenant feeling about nine feet tall.

~~~

Major Thurston and his men with their prisoners had been on the trail for about two hours. They were taking their time, allowing Sergeant O'Malley to catch up with them. They had stopped for a short break when the sentry announced riders coming in. Thurston walked toward the sound of the approaching riders, stopping at the edge of the light from the fire. He heard the sentry challenge the riders and heard O'Malley's Irish brogue when he answered the sentry. Thurston was relieved when he saw that they had two men riding with them. One of them was Dobbs' friend and they shook hands.

"Any problem, Sergeant?"

"Came as meek as a little lamb, Sir." O'Malley answered.

Thurston wondered as he saw the welt under the other man's eye. He smiled. He loved that old Irishman and would be lost without his being around. He depended on him for about everything.

"Break out the biscuits, jerky, and coffee, Sergeant. We might as well stay here for the night and start back early in the morning. See that the prisoners are fed, allowed to relieve themselves one at a time, and then retie their hands and feet. There will be no talking among themselves. Set your sentries and one guard on the prisoners." Thurston walked over to his bedroll and spread it out. He sat down gingerly and cursed under his breath when his butt hit the ground. This was the main reason they were here for the night. His butt would not let him go another mile, hell; he didn't want to go another step. He cursed the man who first invented the army issue saddle and then the man who invented soft office chairs. He then cursed himself again for getting so soft. He lay down on his blanket exhausted, but sleep wouldn't come. His mind was wandering, thinking about that snake Taggart and his whereabouts and whether Delacruz and the patrol had made contact with the Apaches yet. He lay there looking at the twinkling stars and he thought of his ex-wife who he still loved very much. His accepting the job at Fort Clark had cost him his marriage. She could not adapt to the hardships of life on an army outpost. She was used to parties, restaurants, and plenty of stores for shopping back in her hometown of Washington. He loved the army and his command but it had come at a great personal loss.

~~~

Grey Owl was angry beyond control. Where the scout Watkins came from he did not know. Twice in two days this white warrior had ruined his plans and not only cost the lives of many of his warriors but now he had lost the status he had enjoyed only a few hours earlier. He would go back to the Rancheria on the Rio Grande, and then go into the mountains alone and fast for three days. Maybe the Great Spirit, in his great wisdom, would send him a vision on what to do, what the future held. He knew in his heart that he was still destined to do something great for his people, to be talked about in reverence as such warriors as Cochise and Nana were.

For the second time in as many days, he had come close to killing Watkins.   It had been important to him before, but it had now become an obsession with him.   This white man, killer of the Great War chief, Tanza, and his uncle, Lone Wolf, had now killed him, not physically, but his reputation and status with his friends.   The only way he could regain it was to kill this man, this indestructible warrior that had done so much to his people.

Deep down inside of himself, like Tanza and the others, he had great respect for this man. 'He would have made a great warrior, maybe even a chief, if he had been born Apache,' he thought to himself. In spite of himself, he smiled at the thought of what such a warrior could do for his people in their war with the white man. For the present though, he was going to Mexico and the safety of the Rancheria.

THE CROSSING

Chapter XII

As tired as Tye was, instead of going to sleep, he lay on his blanket drinking the last of the coffee that had been in the pot and thinking what he would do if he was in Grey Owl's place.   His pa had taught him this a long time ago. He would tell Tye to put yourself in the person's place you are chasing to see what you would do.   He knew Grey Owl had only four, or five at the most, braves left.   The smart thing to do would be to get back to Mexico and that means, probably at the Rancheria on the Rio Grande.   He thought of several other options, but settled on that.   It would take the better part of two days to get to the Rancheria and he knew the food supplies were running short. This was the big drawback for the army in their fight with the Apaches. The army could go only as long as their supplies held out and the Apaches sometimes took advantage of this. The Apaches traveled light, had food stored all over the country.   The Apaches and their ponies could live off the land if need be, something the soldiers could never do.   A few years earlier, when Tye and his pa were with the Rangers, or Texas Mounted Rifles as some called them, they had good success fighting the Indians because being mostly trappers, hunters, or ex- buffalo hunters, they were used to living off the land. That was then though; the U.S. Army was a different story.

Tye figured the best thing to do was to split the patrol and let him take five or six men and track the Apaches down and let Delacruz take the rest back to the base camp, which was only a full days ride. He could obtain enough rations from the troopers going back for himself and the men with him. They could make them last for three to four days, if they were careful. The only problem now would be to convince Delacruz that it was the best plan. That would have to wait till in the morning.

~~~

Shakespeare had found the San Antonio/San Diego Mail Road and had made great time and had arrived at Fort Davis just at dark. The Suttlers store was closed so he was going to have to spend the night and get his supplies first thing in the morning. He damn near jumped out of his skin when a booming voice hollered.

"HEY, SHAKESPEARE." Shakespeare looked in the direction of the voice and located the source.

"I be dammed," he said. "Lootanant Fetters, is tha yu?"

"Yes sir. It's me."

Shakespeare dismounted and rushed over to the man he had saved from sure death a year earlier up in Colorado, shaking his hand. "Whut are yu doin here, Lootanant"...then he noticed the rank...".I mean Kaptan?"

"Got a transfer and a promotion while I was in the hospital recovering from injuries I got during that fight on the river in Colorado."

"Knu yu got a transfur but didn't kno whare. Kongratulations on tha rank."

"Wasn't for you I wouldn't have it. Hell, I would not even have been alive today." He reached and put his hand on Shakespeare's shoulder and told him to come in the officer's mess hall, get a bite to eat and meet some of the men. Once inside, things quietened down with everyone wondering who the old man in buckskins was. Captain Fetters spoke up.

"Men, this is the man you have heard me talk about. This is the man who saved my sorry carcass up in Colorado. This gentlemen, is the man some of you read about in those novels about the mountain men, Shakespeare McDovitt." All the men got up and came over to shake Shakespeare's hand. Most had read about him and Bridger and the other mountain men and wanted to be able to say they had met one. A thousand questions came at Shakespeare at once. He held up his hand and things got quiet. "I ain't used ta all this tention...its kinder mbarrasing." He paused for a couple seconds. "Okaa, go ahead and make fuuls out uf yurselves," he said smiling, and then laughing with everone else. The questions and handshaking started again.

Most of the questions were concerning Bridger but Shakespeare didn't mind, he was use to that. He was just enjoying answering the questions and remembering those times. A young Lieutenant told everyone to be quiet so he could get a question in.

"Go ahead Lootanant...ask away." Shakespeare said.

"Just how tough was Bridger? I heard a story about him carrying an arrowhead in his butt for a long time. That true?"

"Ta be a monton man wun had ta be pretee damn tugh. Tha's not braggin'...jus a fact. We had no docturs and no medicene, uther than hurbs an home remedees. Ta answur yur queston, Bridger wus as tugh as tha kume...mabee tugher than anywun. He did take an arror high in tha cheek uf his butt. Tha wus in '32, I thank. A French trappe'r got the arror out but tha point staed in. Gave old Jim fitz fur yeers. Like I sade, we didn't have no docturs. In '36 a small wagun train kame into tha Green River kuntry whar we wure havin' our yeerly rondavu. So happ'ns this here train had a boneefide doctur on it and old Jim insisted he take tha arrorhead out. Tha doctur was hesitant about it, tell'n Jim he had nuthing ta kill tha pain. He had examined tha wund and due ta tha lokation and tha amount uf time it had been, knu it wus not as simple as makin an incision and pulling tha arrorhead out. Jim said he kud handle tha pain so jus git it dun. Well, Bridger wus nev'r wun ta pass up an oppertunity ta git a krowd of peeple or make muney...this wus an oppuntunity ta do both. He spred tha wurd around tha kamp about tha opeeration and wus takin' bets he kud handle tha pain an nev'r uttur a wurd. When tha time kame, sum wooden planks wure placed across too wheskey barrells, abut five feet apart fur him ta lie on. Tha men furmed a tite cirkle around tha table at furst, but had ta bac off when tha doctur said he needed mor room. Old Jim's face turned plum red and sweat brok out on his forehead when tha doctur made tha cuts and dug down ta whare tha arrorhead wus lokated."

"When he found tha point, he wus plum upset. He said tha point wus metal, not stone and wus grow'd to tha hip bone. It wuld hav' to be broke off and no wun kuld endure that. Well, ole Jim, knoing he had his whole winter cache uf furs riding, told him ta git to it...and damn quick. Tha old doctur got himself a pare uf big forsups. He klamped down on tha arrorhead and pulled...it didn't kum luse. He klimbed on tha table and straddled Jim and put his wate and muscle to tha task uf breaking it away frum tha bone. Let me tale ya...ole' Jim's eyes wure a bulging, his face turned plum purple, and he bit tha wuden stick in his mouth plum into...but he didn't utter a sound. He passed plum out rite before tha point broke luse. He wus a rich man after kollecting all them furs tha had been bet. If'n he's alive tuday, he will still have tha metal arrorhead hanging round his neck. Tha storee shuld answer yur question, sonny. Jim Bridger wus wun tugh sonufabitch. Wun uther thang abut Bridger wus his sense of humur. He wuld tell tales to them thar tenerfoots tha wuld cum to tha rondervoos we had wunce a yeer. He wuld tell them uf "peetrified" birds tha sang peetrified songs. He wuld tale them uf wenters so kold tha a man had to wait till spring fer his wurds to thaw out so he kuld heer whut he said. He had a reel sense uf humur."

He finally was able to eat. Most had left but Fetters and two of his close friends were still there. Shakespeare had entertained all the men for almost two hours telling stories about those 'shining times'. Most were true, some were stretched some. He learned that from Bridger. He filled Fetters in on the trouble back up the trail with the Indians and about the sheriff from El Paso.

"First trouble we had in awhile. We had several leave the camp and head south a few days ago but we haven't heard of any problems from the forts south of here," Fetters said. "Why in hell's name you going to Clark anyway?"

"If'n you read abut me and Bridger yu had ta reed abut a man named Ben Watkins, tu." Fetters and one of the men nodded their heads. "Wale, his sun Tye, is tha Cheef uf Skouts tha'r and I wunt ta meet him fore I check it in."

"That explains some of the stories we have heard about him. Just a few weeks ago he brought down the Vasquez gang that had robbed the fort's payroll. He then killed an Apache named Tanza and rescued his best friend's grandchildren that Tanza had captured. I guess his pa taught him well."

"Ben wuld du that," Shakespeare said. "Man, I'm plum tucker'd out. Whare can I throw my bedroll fur tha nite?"

"In my quarters, of course," Fetters said.

"Only if'n I can sleep on tha floor. Tried a bed tha uther nite in El Paso and kuldn't go ta sleep. Threw tha blankets on tha floor and slep thar."

The three men smiled and shook their heads. The two friends bid Fetters and Shakespeare goodnight and left. Fetters and Shakespeare retired to his quarters.

~~~

Major Thurston was awakened by a hand shaking his shoulder. He had finally gone to sleep after what seemed like hours and had been sleeping soundly. He opened his eyes to see O'Malley's craggily old face. Raising himself up, he realized everyone else was up and ready to go and he was embarrassed for that. Slipping his boots on and standing up, he let out a low groan and grabbed his butt. The men were watching with amusement etched on their faces.

"Go ahead and laugh," he said... they did. O'Malley brought Thurston's saddled horse over to him with a blanket folded lying on his saddle.

"We thought the padding might help, Major." O'Malley said, trying desperately to keep from laughing again as was every one of the others.

"Very thoughtful of you men," Thurston said as he mounted and sat on the blanket.

"Lead us out, Sergeant," he said. 'This is going to be one long damn day,' he thought to himself as the first jolt of pain hit his butt with his horse's first step. "We may gallop some today but by God, we are not going to trot one step," he thought to himself. Mueller and his men, hands tied behind them, sat on their horses, staring straight ahead, their faces showing no amusement at the Major's problem.

~~~

Tye had been up for awhile and was on his second cup of coffee when Delacruz and Garrison came and sat down beside him.

Garrison shivered. "Getting kinda chilly in the mornings, isn't it.?"

"That's what I love about this country," Tye said. "You can freeze your butt off at night and burn it off during the day."

"Ain't it the truth," Dan August said laughing, as he sat down beside Garrison. He held out his tin cup toward Garrison, who had the coffee pot.

"You have a decision to make, Captain," Tye said. Delacruz looked at Tye.

"What decision?"

Tye took a sip of coffee before speaking. "I checked our supplies last night. We have enough for a day, two at the most. I'm sure that Grey Owl is headed to the Rancheria across the river in Mexico. That's two days traveling and then two back to the wagons at the base camp; four days at the least, and food for two at the most."

"What do you suggest we do then?" Delacruz asked, scratching the back of his neck.

Tye hesitated for a second then laid out his idea. "Give me five men and we'll track down the renegades that are left. You take the rest of the men back to the base camp. They have plenty of supplies there. You can be there by noon tomorrow. Give me and the men with me some of the food you have now and we'll make it last till we end this thing and meet you back at the camp."

"You make it sound so... simple," Delacruz said. "It can't be."

"I'm sure I know where they are headed, but you are right, nothing is ever simple out here. Just about every damn assignment I've ever had has ended up being tough, no matter how simple the orders were," Tye said chuckling. "Seriously though, Captain, we need to end this as soon as possible and this is the best way."

"Do you think five men is enough?"

"Let me pick them and they will be."

Delacruz rubbed the back of his neck, thinking of the pros and cons of Tye's plan. Tye was right about one thing... this needed to be over with and there was no way all the men could go. There was simply not enough supplies. With any man other than Tye, he would not even think about doing it. He knows Apaches and he certainly knows the terrain and what he is doing.

Delacruz stood up. "Pick your men, Tye. I'll gather what supplies I can for you.

Tye stood up just as Lieutenant Rogers walked up with a sheepish grin on his face.

"What's the grin about so early in the morning, Lieutenant?" Tye asked, shaking his hand.

Rogers hesitated for a second or two. "This is an embarrassing situation, Tye."

Tye looked him in the eye and had a big grin on

his face. "Let me guess. With Franks dead, as well as your scout, you're in unfamiliar territory and you're not sure how to get back to Inge."

Rogers looked at the ground and kicked it and nodded his head.

"Nothing to be embarrassed about, Lieutenant. The Captain and me have already discussed it. You will go back to the camp with Delacruz. He will send a rider to Fort Clark with a dispatch for Major Thurston. You can send a man with him and he can get a fresh mount there and go on to Inge with your dispatch."

"You figured I was lost."

"I figured you was but I didn't know if any of your men had been out here this far west from Inge and could find their way back. Just remember one thing when and if this happens again. You will always be north or south of the Old Mail Road, regardless of where you are. Head toward the road and sooner or later you will hit it. It will take you home. You learn, Lieutenant, everyday you are out here. Learn and remember. You proved to me yesterday that you have what it takes to make it in this country."

"I'll remember, Thanks." They shook hands and Tye turned to give his list of men he wanted to Delacruz. Delacruz looked at it for a minute,

"That's just about the same as I would have chosen. I'll find them, tell them they have volunteered for a special assignment," he said laughing. Tye walked to the picket line and threw his blanket and saddle on Sandy. He had already checked his pistol and rifle, so he rolled a smoke while waiting on the men to show up. He was almost thru with his smoke when he saw them coming.

"What the hell did I volunteer for this time, Tye?" Phipps said with that ever present grin spread across his face.

"Just another exciting adventure where you have a good chance to die," Tye said smiling back.

"Sure wouldn't want to volunteer for anything boring," Phipps said, shaking Tye's hand. Billy August, Lieutenant Garrison, Sergeant Anderson, and Corporal Langston all walked up and gathered around Tye.

I'll make it short and simple," Tye told them. "I'm sure Grey Owl has headed for the Rancheria on the Rio Grande, which is about two good days ride from here. Our supplies will not allow the whole column to go. Captain Delacruz is gathering some extra supplies for us. He will take the column back to the base camp while I am going after Grey Owl, along with you... my volunteers." He grinned and added, "Any questions?" No one said anything. "Anyone not want to go?" Again, no reply.

"Good. We'll be leaving before daylight so get your gear and check your weapons. If you are short on ammunition, let me know before we leave. I'll meet you back here with the horses in twenty minutes." He walked to where Delacruz was taking stock of the supplies from the rest of the men.

"We're pretty short, Tye."

Tye looked at the supplies and there was less than he figured.

"Will this help?" Lieutenant Rogers said, laying a sack containing jerky and coffee on the ground."I gathered what I could from my men. Least we can do for ya'll saving our hides."

"This will do, Lieutenant. Thanks," a grateful Tye said shaking the lieutenant's hand. Tye gathered up the supplies. "I'll see you in four or so days, Captain." He shook Delacruz's hand and turned, walking back to where Sandy and the other horses were.

He was pleased to find the men waiting, anxious to leave. Tye walked over to Sandy, put the coffee and some jerky in his saddle bags and gave Garrison a like amount to put into his. "Ready, Lieutenant?"

"We're ready," Tye mounted Sandy, turned him, and over his shoulder said. "Let's do it then." He kicked Sandy and headed out with his scout, Dan, beside him and the rest following, just as the gray light of dawn was breaking.

~~~

Grey Owl and his men were breaking camp. It had been a long two days and last night was the longest he could remember. One of the wounded men with him had died during the night. Two more were wounded and one of them, his best friend Spotted Antelope, was in a bad way. The other had a leg wound but was managing to stay on his pony. They had lost a lot of time taking care of the one who had died and with his friend, Spotted Antelope. His friend was suffering a lot from the stomach wound and could stay on his mount only with help. Trotting or running the ponies was out of the question.   He knew Watkins was probably closing the gap between them with him going so slow because of his friend. There was no chance of escaping the scout. They would probably meet later today, no later than tomorrow.

His killing Watkins was the only thing that could save his status. His hopes of being one of the great warriors of the Apache had passed... unless he could do this. Two suns ago, he had over forty warriors, now he had three that could fight and one that would probably die, all because of this man.   He hated him; he hated everything about him; yet strangely, he admired him.

He now believed the old men of the tribe; the free life of the Apache was over. No longer would they be free to hunt and raid as their fathers had done for all these years. If the Apache were to survive, they would have to accept the fact they could not win against the advancing white man, and try to live in peace with him. He rode his paint, not proud with his head held high like he did a couple days ago, but with shoulders slumped and head down.

~~~

It was mid afternoon when the patrol, led by Major Thurston, crossed the bridge over Los Moras Creek and entered the Fort. He ordered the prisoners taken to the guardhouse and he went to his office. He saluted the orderly when he entered.

"Anything I need to take care of this minute?" he asked his weariness showing in his voice.

"No Sir," answered the orderly.

"Good. Would you get my Adjutant, Captain McClain, to come to my office?"

"Yes Sir. Right away, Sir," the orderly replied.

Thurston entered his office, threw his hat on the chair by the wall and gently sat down in his soft, cushioned chair. The soft leather felt wonderful on his sore, chaffed butt and he cursed the McClellan saddle for the ten thousandth time, or ever how many steps his damn horse took the last two days. He leaned back, closed his eyes and totally relaxed every muscle in his body. He decided he would have a hot bath later instead of the usual bath in the creek. He dozed and was awaken by the orderly knocking on his door, announcing that Captain McClain was here. Thurston sat up in the chair, straighten his tunic and ran his fingers thru his salt and pepper hair.

"Come in."

The orderly stepped in, saluted and announced McClain.

Thurston wearily returned the salute as McClain entered. "Come over and sit down, Captain. I need to get some correspondence out immediately."

"Yes Sir," McClain answered, taking some paper and a pen out of his ever present, black leather folder that the men jokingly said was permanently attached to his hand. McClain had heard the remarks but paid them no mind. He knew his job was not fighting Apaches and bandits, but making sure that all the correspondence and personnel records were up to date and in order. He was very good at his job and he was appreciated by Thurston.

"I need to send a dispatch to General Reynolds, The Fifth Military District Commander in San Antonio."

"Yes Sir. I'm ready, Sir."

After dictating the letter, McClain handed it to him to read and make any changes he deemed necessary. Thurston sat back in his chair and looked over the dispatch. He wished the telegraph was available out here but as of now the lines were not this far west; they stopped at San Antonio.

General James Reynolds
09/OCT/68
Fifth Military District Commander
San Antonio, Texas

Sir:
Recent events here have been brought to my attention and it is something you should be aware of. Most of the trouble with the Apaches has led to the fact that Mr. Taggart, the government agent, has been taking most of the

supplies, including the cattle that was assigned for the Apaches, and selling them for his personal profit. We have his partners in the guardhouse here at Clark.

In the last six months, an untold number of homesteaders have been killed, nineteen troopers and scouts killed, and many more wounded by the Apaches. Not sure how many apaches have been killed, but it would be a significant number. Taggart might as well have killed all of them himself. He has left and his whereabouts is unknown at this time. He is a small man but is traveling with a man that is six foot three plus and about two hundred fifty pounds. Taggart has never been seen in anything but a black suit and string tie, with a black hat. He could be heading toward San Antonio. I am also advising by dispatch, the commander of Fort Inge to be on the lookout for him

A search for a new agent, an honest one, should be started. I have one of my sergeants at the camp, now, taking care of things. I have given the old chief some of my cattle as a sign of good will.

My Chief of Scouts, Tye Watkins is currently in pursuit of a large band of Apaches that have killed several homesteaders. Hopefully, an honest agent that will keep our promises to the Apaches will put an end to the uprisings.

Your Obedient Servant,

Major James Thurston
Post Commander
Fort Clark, Texas

Thurston read it again, signed it, and dismissed Captain McClain with the instructions to have a dispatch rider on the way within the hour to San Antonio. He stood up, walked over to the wall map and briefly studied it, wondering where Delacruz was. He could only pray everything was all right. Right now, he wanted to rest, so he walked over to the couch and stretched out. He was asleep immediately.

~~~

Rebecca had finished cleaning the house... again. She sat on the porch trying to think of something else to do. The only way she could keep her mind off Tye was to stay busy. The daytime wasn't to bad because she had some of the other wives to visit with but at night, when she was alone, she would cry herself to sleep. Mrs. O'Malley told her it would get better; she would learn to get use to it... but she wasn't so sure. It may get a little easier, but it was always going to be lonely. God, she missed him...missed his arms around her, his lips on hers, his gentle touch. It amazed her that a man like Tye, so tough, so lethal when need be, could be so gentle and loving.

Chapter XIII

Mid afternoon found Tye and Dan standing beside the shallow grave where the Apache lay.

"They were in a hurry to bury him. Not a proper way for an Apache to go to the spirit world," Dan said, looking at the way the Apaches buried this young warrior, barely covering him with rocks. Tye nodded in agreement and turned as Garrison and the men rode up.

"Looks like they are down to four or five, Lieutenant, and from the looks of the tracks heading out, they still have at least one who's having a hard time staying in the saddle." Garrison dismounted, and walked over to the stare at the dead warrior. "How far behind are we?"

Tye looked in the direction the tracks were headed. "Maybe three, four hours."

Garrison looked shocked. "That close?" he said questionly.

"They haven't been able to make very good time, Lieutenant," Dan said. "They won't till they leave the wounded one behind or he dies."

All heads jerked around when shots were heard south of them, and not far away. "Take a look, Dan and report back," Tye ordered.

"What do you think it is?"

"Ain't the Apaches we're chasing and I haven't heard of any others loose. There's a homestead a mile or so in that direction. My guess would be border bandits raiding it. Let's be ready to ride when Dan gets back."

~~~

Kyle Bates, along with his teenage sons, Bill and Frank, lay behind the over turned table on the porch of their home. His wife, Martha, and daughter, Mary, were in the house. All their eyes were on the body of the oldest son, Jesse, who lay in the afternoon sun, a bullet in his back. He wasn't dead and Kyle had hollered at him not to move too much or they would shoot him again. The shots had come from the rocks about sixty yards away.

They were in a pretty good defensive position. Kyle was no greenhorn when he came out here and he had picked a good spot. The back of the cabin was almost against a seventy foot vertical cliff that had an overhang at the top, which sheltered the cabin during the heat of the day. The barn and stable were a short distance north of the house, keeping the stable smell downwind from the prevailing southwest wind. They had a good line of fire to keep intruders away from the house. There was nothing but open spaces to the left, or south of the house. No place to hide for two hundred yards. He always figured if trouble came, it would be from the front. He was right.

Sitting in the shade of the large rocks, Manuel Estrada and his gang of cutthroats studied the situation. The surprise attack didn't go as well as planned, only because some of his men were poor shots. The men at the house were all in the open and only one was hit. This was his first attack in Texas. The heat from the Federalist in Mexico had forced him to cross over into Texas. He had thirteen men with him and they needed the supplies that would be in this house. He was pondering what to do. The men on the porch were in a good defensive position but he was betting they had only single shot rifles. They would have time to fire once, maybe twice, before his horses could cover the distance between where he was and the house. He had studied them for awhile before firing the shots. He knew the old man was probably pretty handy and steady with a gun, but the other two looked awful young. He was turning over the odds in his head of how many men would be hit. He looked behind him and smiled. The sun would be setting in about an hour and would be in the eyes of those on the porch. He could wait.

~~~

Dan had studied the situation and was reporting to Tye and Lieutenant Garrison. "There's fifteen or so Mexican bandits and they have a man and his kids pinned down on the porch of their homestead. One man is down in the yard. Don't know who's in the house. I figure they are waiting till the setting sun will be in their eyes to make their move."

"Damn," Tye said. Helping these people was going to let the Apaches increase the distance between them, but Tye couldn't let a family die for that reason. He turned to Garrison. "We're out here to protect these people. I know this diminishes our chances of catching Grey Owl, but what choice do we have?"

"What the hell are we waiting for?" Phipps chimed in. Everyone agreed, so they headed out, Dan leading the way.

Ten minutes later, Tye and Dan lay on the crest of a hill, looking down at the backs of the bandits two hundred yards in front and below them. They could see the house about sixty or seventy yards past the bandits.

"How we gonna handle this?" Dan whispered.

"Looks like we have only one choice and that's to hit them now, before they rush the house." They slid back down the hill to where the men waited.

"What's the situation?" Garrison asked.

"Not good," Tye answered. "We will have to hit them from behind. Hopefully, with their attention on the house they won't know we are there till it's too late. If they see us, it's gonna get rough."

August chipped in, "At least the sun will be at our backs just like those scum figured it would be on theirs. That'll help our chances."

Garrison nodded and looked at the men, then at Tye. "Mounted or on foot?"

"We have a better chance of surprising them on foot."

"Dismount men. Corporal Langston, you and Phipps set the picket line there," Garrison ordered, pointing to two large mesquites that were far enough apart to run a rope and hold the horses. With that done, they moved to get in position.

"They will be looking at the house so being quiet is absolutely necessary," Tye said. They were a hundred fifty yards behind the bandits and were approaching them ten yards apart in a skirmish line. Tye and Garrison were in the middle with Dan, and Langston and Sergeant Anderson on the ends. They were moving almost at a trot, watching the bandits and being careful not to trip or make any more noise than necessary. At eighty yards, Tye signaled them to walk. At that instant, one of the bandits signaled the others and they stood up and prepared to rush the house. As they did, they were startled to see the soldiers at their backs.

"Kneel and fire," Garrison ordered.

They did and it showed why Tye picked these men. They were steady in a tight situation and they were good shots. Five bandits went down with the first volley. After firing, they dropped their rifles and charged, running not in a straight line but going left then right with their pistols out, not giving the bandits a good target. The bandits recovered from the shock of seeing the troopers and from the devastating rain of death that came with the first volley, and returned fire of their own.

Kyle Bates and the boys were as surprised as Estrada and his gang were when they saw the soldiers approaching. A hopeless situation had suddenly turned into maybe, a positive one. When the bandits turned to face the rushing troopers after the first volley from the soldiers, Kyle and his boys cut loose with their rifles. Kyle was an old mountain man and was an excellent shot and he had taught the boys well. Three more bandits went down with bullets in their backs.

The bullets were zipping around Tye and the others. Tye heard the all familiar thud of one hitting flesh, followed by a grunt, but did not turn to see who was hit. They were about forty yards from the bandits when they stopped and fired their pistols, two or three rounds each. More bandits went down but not before another volley of bullets came their way. One nicked Tye on the upper left arm and he heard another thud and grunt from behind and to his left. Another volley from the remaining soldiers and from the Bates, and the bandits that were left, dropped their guns and held their hands over their heads.

Tye motioned them to come forward. When they were away from the rocks, he motioned them to lay on the ground, which they did. Tye turned to see Garrison, Dan, and Phipps coming in behind him.

"Phipps, you and Dan watch these bastards," Garrison said, turned and with Tye, went back where they had been to check on Anderson and Langston. They found Langston, dead, shot square in the chest. Sergeant Anderson was lucky even though he was hit twice, once in the leg and once in the shoulder. The bullet in the leg had gone clean thru, missing the bone, but the one in the shoulder had struck bone and was still there. Tye picked him up easily and carried him back to the others. Garrison, struggling some with the limp body of Langston, did the same.

Kyle Bates was checking on his wounded son. "He's okay, just hurting some," he said to his other sons. "Ya'll get him in the house where your ma can patch him up and then come out here to meet these here soldiers that just saved our butts."

When Tye and Garrison arrived with the injured man and Langston, the Bates were there slapping Phipps's and Dan's backs. The old man walked over and shook Garrison's hand and then walked to where Tye was. "You have to be Watkins," he exclaimed, shaking Tye's hand vigorously. "Been hearing about you for years. Met your pa a couple times."

"Where did you know my pa from?"

"Trapped beaver for a couple seasons in the Yellowstone. Met him a couple times at rendezvous time. He was a hell of a mountain man. I was just a pup at the time. I got in at the end, only got to trap three years. He turned and introduced his sons to Tye.

"Figured you wasn't no greenhorn," Tye said to Bates, while shaking his son's hands. "You picked a good spot to build. I saw a man down in your yard. He okay?"

"My oldest son. He's hit, but I think he'll be okay. Your man there needs some doctoring. Bring him into the house. My wife is a good hand at patching up wounds. God knows she has had enough practice, "he said laughing. It was easy for him to laugh now, and he did. His oldest will be okay and the rest of his family had just been snatched from the jaws of death. 'Yes sir, it was going to end up being a great day considering what it could have been,' he thought to himself.

"Bring him in and lay him on the bed over there," Bates said to Tye and Garrison, who had carried Anderson into the modest homestead. Tye, as they lay Anderson on the bed, had already noticed this was a well kept home. The wooden floor was swept clean, the table was covered by a clean cloth, all the dishes were washed, and very little dust could be seen. Everything was in its place. All signs of a happy and healthy home.

"This is my wife, Martha," Kyle said introducing Tye and Garrison. Both tipped their hats and said "mam" at the same time. She was a typical frontier woman; not real attractive but of strong body, mind and spirit. In a lot of ways, the women out here were tougher than their men. They made homes for their families from little or nothing. Most had dirt floors and homemade furniture and not much of it. They had to be lover, mother, doctor, housekeeper, and sometimes had to fight for their families when their man was gone or dead. Some think the toughest was that they seldom had another woman to talk to. They were a special breed, just like their men.

168

Martha was looking at Anderson's wound and barking orders to her children to get this and get that. She had already patched her oldest. The bullet had gone clean thru him without hitting bone or a vital organ. He had been very lucky.

"The bullet isn't going to kill him but it's got to come out now or he will start running a fever that can kill him," Martha said speaking of Anderson's wound. Listening to her, Tye could tell she knew what she was doing and motioned to Garrison to follow him outside.

"Lieutenant, we have got to get after Grey Wolf but we have a big problem."

"What now?" Garrison asked.

"We have one dead and one wounded. You have five prisoners that will slit your throat in a second if you aren't careful." Tye hesitated a moment before going on. "This is what I think we need to do. Dan can lead you and Phipps back to the camp with Anderson and the prisoners. I need to get after Grey Wolf now."

"ALONE?" An astonished Garrison asked.

"Alone," Tye said. "There's no way one or two men can get the prisoners and Anderson back. When you get back to camp, get some supplies and Dan can lead you to the Rancheria on the Rio Grande where I think the Apaches are headed. I can stay on top of them, keep track of them, and leave a trail Dan can follow if they don't stay there. Course, they could go deep into Mexico and all is for naught."

Garrison paused for a second, looking Tye in the eye. "You sure this is a good plan?"

"I think it's the only chance of catching the renegades. It will probably be tomorrow before you can move Anderson. That would eliminate all chance of catching them."

"PHIPPS," Garrison hollered.

Phipps came running.   "Yes, sir."

"Get Mr. Watkins's horse, extra rations for him and oats for Sandy."

"Yes Sir."

Ten minutes later, Tye was on his way. Garrison wondered if he had made a mistake in letting him go, but Tye was right in his reasoning.   It was the only way.   Another simple plan that would not be so simple in the end.   He stood there watching Tye ride off in the fading light.   He had a bad feeling about this and he remembered what Tye had told him about feelings. "Take care Tye," He uttered under his breath. He went back into the house to see if he could help with Anderson's wounds.   He found out quickly Anderson was in good hands.   Mrs. Bates had removed the bullet and patched both wounds.   Anderson was sleeping soundly.

"Few shots of good whiskey works every time," she said laughing.   "I'll have us something to eat shortly."

"That's not necessary, Mrs. Bates."

"That's the least we can do for what ya'll did," she said.   "Did the one that was killed have a family?"

"No mam', he didn't," Phipps said.   "He was just a soldier.   Onliest family he had as far as I know was us, his fellow troopers."   She nodded her head. "What was his name?"

"Langston, mam... Billy Langston."

"Langston," she repeated.   "We'll remember him in our prayers."   She went back to fixing the meal.

Garrison and Bates went outside and sat on the porch.   Garrison told Phipps as soon as he had eaten to take Dan's place watching the prisoners so he could eat.   "I heard you tell Tye you knew his father," Garrison said.

"Didn't   know   him   well;   met   him   at   the

170

rendezvous a couple of times."

"I heard he was quite a man," Garrison commented.

"He ran traps with Jim Bridger, and Shakespear McDovitt. To do that, you had to be good cause no one was better than Bridger and his group. Ben, that's Tye's father's name, made a name for himself with his fighting ability. He never lost a wrestling match or a stand up knock'um down fist fight at the rendezvous. He killed several Blackfeet in hand to hand fights with knives and tomahawks. Even had some stories written about his exploits by some eastern writer. From what I hear, Tye is just like him."

Garrison laughed. "There's not a one of us at Fort Clark whose rear he hasn't saved at least once. He's good alright...real good. I guess I know now where he learned all his skills." He thought to himself that Tye was going to need all those skills against four or five upset Apaches that knew he was tracking them.

Chapter XIV

Tye had picked up the tracks of the Apaches just before full dark. He knew the only way he could catch them would be to keep moving all night. He wouldn't be able to see the tracks but he still felt they were heading for the Rancheria. He knew a way that would knock off two or three hours and apparently the young bucks he was chasing didn't know of it. He suddenly felt better. He felt he had a chance of catching up before they crossed the river. He turned Sandy away from the tracks and toward the shortcut he and his pa had used years earlier.

The long forgotten landmarks were coming back to him as he moved under a bright, full moon. Even Sandy seemed relaxed and enjoying the new country and the coolness of traveling in the night air.

"Damn near as bright as day, Sandy. Glad the Apaches went another route cause with this moon, picking off a lonely old scout wouldn't be hard to do." He patted Sandy on the neck. "Kinda enjoying this cool air, huh old boy?" Sandy nickered and shook his head, proving again to a smiling Tye what he already knew... Sandy understood every word he said.

Sandy suddenly stopped, bucked once and then danced sideways damn near throwing Tye off.

"WHOA, BOY. WHOA," he shouted, jerking hard on the reins. He got Sandy under control and saw the source of the problem and was glad he didn't get thrown. "That's the biggest damn rattlesnake I ever saw." The rattler, coiled and angry, was as thick as Tye's upper arm and over five feet long. Tye guided Sandy away from it and continued on his way, thankful that he, Sandy, and the snake was none the worse for the meeting.

As the night wore on and the trail grew more familiar, old memories crept into Tye's mind. Memories of the good times he and his pa had experienced many years before on this trail and so many others. As he thought some about it, seemed he and Ben spent more nights under the stars than under their roof. Maybe that's why, until he met Rebecca, he had always been more comfortable on the trail than cooped up in a house. Listening to Ben's stories when he trapped with Bridger and Shakespear during the 'shining times' of the mountain men made him wish he had been born fifty years earlier.

The night went quickly and as the sky was turning gray he stopped at a spring to rest Sandy and himself. He figured he had made up hours on the Apaches and had time to rest some. He and Sandy may need all their strength before this day was over. He loosened the girth on the saddle, gave Sandy some oats and water before he ate some jerky and lay down on the short grama grass that surrounded the spring, shut his eyes and was immediately asleep. He would depend on Sandy to alert him of anyone or anything coming around.

~~~

Spotted Antelope was in a bad way this morning. Grey Owl did not sleep much as he was in a quandary as to what to do...leave his friend here to die alone or take him with them and travel at a very slow pace, which would probably end up getting all of them killed. He was sure Watkins was on their trail and probably not far behind. Just the thought of this white man made his blood boil.

He would take his friend with him. He turned to the others. "Put him on his pony and tie his feet to each other. Spotted Antelope," he said shaking his friends shoulder. "Can you hold on to your pony's mane?" Spotted Antelope nodded his head. When they stood him up, it caused him some pain but it barely showed in the expression on his face. This was typical of the Apache, showing no pain. Grey Owl placed his hand on his friends shoulder, looked him in the eye and nodded. The others placed him on his horse and tied a rope on one foot and ran it under the horse's belly and tied it to the other foot pulling it snug. Spotted Antelope looked at his friend, managed a slight smile, grabbed a handful of mane and kicked his pony in motion. Grey Wolf, along with the others jumped on theirs and chased after him.

The chase brought back memories, good memories, of the races he and Spotted Antelope had enjoyed; running free, the wind in their face, and not a care in the world. This was before the flood of the white eyes that had changed their way of life. It looks like that change was forever. Spotted Antelope looked back and Grey Owl thought he saw a smile on his friends face as he closed the gap between them. When he pulled along the side of Spotted Antelope, he was shocked to see his friend's face... set in death. His hands still gripped his pony's mane but his eyes were lifeless, open but seeing nothing. Grey Owl reached over and grabbed the rope halter and pulled the horse to a stop. Once stopped, his friend fell to the side and was caught by Grey Owl.

"Untie my friend's feet and lay him down on the ground...gently." When this was done, he sat on the ground and cradled his friend's head in his lap. Looking to the sky he asked the Great Spirit to take him into his care. He said that Spotted Antelope was a good Apache, a great warrior that had taken many enemy scalps. They did not have time to bury him proper but scooped out a shallow grave and laid him in it and then placed flat rocks on him to keep the coyotes away. They mounted their ponies, and with only a quick look back at where his friend lay, Grey Owl led them away, toward the Rancheria.

~~~

The sun was over the top of the hills when Tye opened his eyes. He figured he slept about an hour and a half and he felt better but he knew fatigue from lack of sleep would catch up with him later, especially when the sun was high and the temperature was rising. He tightened the saddle girth on Sandy, mounted him and headed west. He figured he would be there by noon and to the best of his figuring, the Apaches slowed by the wounded, would be there maybe by mid afternoon, sunset at the latest.

The terrain here was not too difficult but he could see the steep cliffs in the not to far distance where travel would be much more difficult. The hills were gorgeous, at least in his eyes. Most men looked at it as arid waste land and worthless, but to Tye and the large number of homesteaders, it was home and it was beautiful. The green cedars and cactus were in stark contrast to the light grayish blue of the purple sage. Now and in the spring was Tye's favorite time of the year, not too hot and not too cold. Even Sandy was showing his feisty nature this morning; Tye had to hold him to a trot.

The miles went by quickly and they were soon in

the steep hills close to the river.   His path now was all too familiar...rough and tough on both horse and rider. At times the trail was barely wide enough for Sandy to squeeze past the boulders and the flesh tearing cactus that grew from the cracks in them.   "Like I said before, Sandy, everything out here can scratch, stick, or sting you," Tye said patting him on the neck.

About half past noon he saw the bluff that overlooked the Rio Grande and the Apache Rancheria on the other side.   Out of habit, Tye walked Sandy off the trail a short distance, gave him some water and left him in the shade of a high cliff.   He took his canteen and rifle and made his way up the bluff.   It was fairly steep and was remarkably clean of loose rocks and pebbles.   "This would be one hot place in the summer," he mumbled to himself.

At the top, he looked over the rim down at the slow moving river that served as the Border between Texas and Mexico. There had been little rain this year and now, the river was low.   The last time he was here, the river was deep and swift. Looking across the river he saw that the Rancheria was empty. He slid back down the slope and hurried over to where Sandy was.

"We beat'um," he said patting Sandy on the neck.   "We beat them here, Sandy."   His plan was now to move about a mile downstream where there was a crossing.   He wanted to catch them on this side of the river and that was the only place that a man could safely cross for a long ways up or down the river. He was sure that was where he would find them. He mounted Sandy and headed for the crossing downstream, feeling a new surge of energy flowing thru his body.

~~~

Back at Fort Clark, everyone was staying clear of Major Thurston who was in a bad mood. Not only was he mad, he was worried, and his butt still hurt. He had spoken with Meechum and the prisoners twice and no one was talking about where that scum Taggart might be. He was worried about the troop he had sent to bring back Grey Owl. He had not heard from them. He was still cursing himself for letting his butt get so soft.

He had sent small patrols in every direction searching for Taggart, to no avail. The only good news lately was that a shipment of cattle had come from San Antonio for the Indians. When they had been delivered to the Apache camp, there had been much celebrating. Thurston's interpreter, who had gone with the detail to the camp with the cattle, came back with the news that the old Chief had given Thurston a new name. Translated into English, it was *'He Who Talks Straight'.* Thurston had to smile at that and the thought crossed his mind that maybe after Grey Owl was corralled or dead, things might just settle down...at least for awhile anyway.

As far as finding Taggart, he figured that would happen when Tye returned. He intended to let Tye speak with Meechum...alone. He smiled at that thought, as he remembered a couple months ago when he let Tye in the cell with one of the Vasquez's gang members. Thurston had not been able to get any information from the prisoner. He was restricted as to what he could do to get it. He told Tye that he had no control over things he did not know about, so he left Tye alone with the Mexican. Tye got the information and the Fort's surgeon was called to the cell the next morning to doctor the prisoner's mysterious injuries. Thurston smiled at that thought.

~~~

Tye could see the cut between the cliffs that led to the river crossing.   He was sitting on Sandy about a half mile away.   Looking to the east, across the almost flat landscape, he could see nothing moving except a couple of buzzards floating lazily high above the ground.   He looked back toward the terrain he had to cross to get to the notch and he didn't like it.   It was mostly flat with waist high cedar, cactus, and sage...not much cover and he sure as hell didn't relish the idea of getting caught out there by four or so Apaches.

Studying the lay of the land a little closer, he noticed a draw that looked like it went almost all the way to the cut.   He knew this part of the country was laced by hundreds of such draws that was cut thru the dirt and rocks over the years by runoffs of heavy rains; most ended up emptying into the river.   This particular draw looked about five or six foot deep.   It was enough to conceal him on foot but not sitting on Sandy.   He thought about it for a moment then made his decision. He walked Sandy over to the base of a cliff that would keep him in the shade for the rest of the day.   There was a little grama grass he could munch on while Tye was gone.

Taking his canteen and rifle, Tye dropped into the draw.   He was jogging with the easy, relaxed gait of an Apache.   The floor of the draw was sandy and remarkably smooth...and damp from a recent runoff. Tye noticed he was leaving tracks that could be followed by even a half blind Apache.   He had been jogging for a couple of minutes when he stopped, standing frozen like a statue for a few seconds. Men like him had a special sense that warned them of impending danger.   He had just had one of those feelings go thru him.

He found a place to get out of the draw and removing his hat, looked over the tops of the sage and cedars. "Damn," he said disgustingly. The Apaches, four of them, were about two hundred yards away and coming almost directly at him. Dropping back into the draw, Tye hurriedly backtracked where he had come from. After about a hundred yards he stopped to check where they were. Climbing out, he again looked over the tops of the brush. He felt better by what he saw...they were going to miss where he had been by a few yards so they would not see his tracks.

His thinking he was safe ended quickly. One of the Apaches stopped, dismounted and walked over to the draw to relieve his bladder. The others kept going after hollering something at the brave...probably Apache ribbing. Tye held his breath, the damn brave was standing on the exact spot he had been a few minutes ago. As he watched, he could tell by the Apaches body language he had spotted the tracks. The Apache looked down the draw where Tye was. Tye looked away, not wanting the Apache to feel he was being watched. A fighting man could sometimes feel it when someone was staring at him.

The Apache was coming, walking on the side of the draw, following the tracks. Tye was in a fix now. If he shot the warrior, the others would be coming. He had to look for some way, or something, to give him an edge and allow him to kill him without firing a shot. He was at a fast walk when the 'something' showed its face... an indention in the smooth walls of the draw got his attention. It was on the same side the Apache was walking on and was deep enough for him to get inside and not be seen from above.

He walked a ways past the place and then carefully retraced his steps, walking backwards, being careful to step exactly in his old tracks.   If the Apache fell for this, he would walk past Tye following the tracks, and then could be surprised from behind. The plan sounded simple enough but Tye knew nothing was ever simple and nothing ever went exactly as planned. Backing to the indention and after considerable work, got his six foot two, one hundred ninety pounds into it...he waited, sweating. It seemed like a long time but was actually probably only a couple of minutes before he saw the Apache's shadow in the draw, moving slowly toward him.   Tye held his breath, his heart pounding.   He knew he was a dead man if his plan did not work, what with his being in this hole, barely able to move.   The shadow stopped, the Apache was directly above him.   Tye knew the warrior was sensing something was wrong and Tye was just fixing to leap out and take his chances when the shadow moved on. Tye breathed a sigh of relief and waited a little longer to make his move.

Chapter XV

Tye quietly slipped out of the indention and took two quick steps, his feet making no sound on the soft sand. The Apache sensing something, turned to look behind him just as Tye swung his rifle intending to knock the braves legs out from under him. The Apache, with reflexes like a cat, jumped in the air and the rifle went past, under his feet. However, when he came down he was on the edge of the draw and lost his balance, falling into the draw hitting hard on his back. Tye was on him quicker than you could blink, intending to drive his Bowie into the brave's chest. He was surprised when a hand shot up and with a grip like a steel trap, stopped the downward thrust and held it. Tye barely caught the Apaches other hand which had appeared with a knife. They rolled over a couple of times, neither gaining an advantage over the other.

They managed to get to their feet, still locked together in their struggle to jerk their hands free from the other. The Apache tried to knee Tye in the groin but Tye, wise to that old trick, turned his hips and caught the blow on his left hip. In retaliation, Tye lowered his head, and gathering himself, viciously butted the Apache in the face. Tye's hand came free and he drove the blade deep into the chest of the Apache. The warrior stood looking at Tye, his black eyes that were full of fire and hate a second ago locked onto Tye's. He tried to say something but only a bloody froth dribbled from his lips and mingled with the blood that ran from his smashed nose. His black eyes dimmed and then set as life left him and he crumbled to the ground, his lifeless eyes staring at but not seeing the blue sky. Tye sat down hard on the sand, breathing hard from the fight.

He lay back on the sand, propped up on his elbows, head back, sucking precious air into his lungs, thankful to still be alive. "For just a youngster, that young buck was the quickest, strongest I've seen in a while," he said while gulping in air. He was feeling the effects of the lack of sleep from last night. He rested for two more minutes, stood up, found his hat and placed it back on his head. He picked up his rifle, checked it for blockage, stuck his Bowie into the sand to get the blood off and then wiped it on the dead Apache's breechcloth. He hurried to where Sandy was, mounted him, and headed for the cut. Apparently, the other Apaches were not curious about why their friend had not caught up to them as they were nowhere in sight, which was okay with Tye.

Arriving at the narrow cut between the cliffs that led to the crossing, Tye pulled Sandy up and sat there for a minute studying the situation. He wanted to make damn sure there was no surprise waiting for him from Grey Owl. Walking Sandy into the cut, he could see the tracks of the three ponies entering the cut and farther on, into the water. This was the same crossing he had caught Lone Wolf and Tanza by hiding in the brush on the Mexican side, catching them when they came out of the water. He was leary of one, or all of the Apaches, doing the same to him.

Tye had a reputation of always knowing exactly what to do in any situation, but right now he wasn't sure. He felt sure they knew he would be following them and if he was Grey Owl, he would set a trap. Tye looked at the sun which was almost touching the tops of the cliffs, meaning full dark wasn't but an hour or so away. He was thinking he might just wait on this side to see if they come back across looking for their friend since it would be dark soon, or he could play it safe, and head back to the base camp and wait for another day to catch Grey Owl. He was here now so he discarded that idea quickly, choosing to try and end it here and now.

He walked Sandy about two hundred yards back in a draw and picketed him in a patch of grama grass. He poured some water in his hat and gave Sandy a good drink.

"May be a long night feller," he said as he gave Sandy his favorite thing, a good scratching high on his forehead, between the ears. Sandy shook his head and nuzzled Tye. "I'll see you in the morning, old boy." Tye walked back to the cut to find a place that would be out of sight and prepared to wait... probably all night.

~~~

Rebecca had just left the O'Malley's and was walking toward the creek to where their home was. She had spent the afternoon visiting Mrs. O'Malley and the Turley children. Her new home was down by the creek-but empty-Tye was still gone. The Turley children had been the grandkids of Tye's good friends, Jim and Marie Turley. The kids had been abducted by Tanza and his band after murdering Jim and Marie and their son and daughter in law. Tye had brought them back after killing Tanza, and the O'Malley's, whose

184

children were grown, had adopted them.

     Rebecca's day had not been good. It was one of those days when she missed Tye even more than normal. She spent the early part of the day crying and finally went to see Mrs. O'Malley. Mrs. O'Malley had been thru the same thing for years with Sergeant O'Malley always gone on patrol and also the years he was fighting in the war between the North and the South. She understood completely Rebecca's feelings and always seemed to know exactly what to say or do to cheer her up. Today was no exception and Rebecca was walking home feeling much better about things and more appreciative than ever for Mrs. O'Malley. She had thought of her parents a lot lately. She wished they were still alive to meet Tye. They were loving people and would have made great grandparents. She fixed her a bite to eat, washed what dishes she could find dirty, went outside on the porch for awhile, then went in to go to bed...once again, by herself. She said her usual nightly prayer, asking God to protect Tye and to bring him back to her safely. She lay down and cried herself to sleep.

~~~

     The sun had dropped behind the hills and Tye was struggling to stay awake. A cool breeze made the temperature perfect...for sleeping. "Go to sleep now old boy and you might get a long one if the Apaches slip up on you." He wished he had some strong cavalry coffee. "That damn stuff will sure as hell keep you awake." He thought of a patrol he was on when Corporal Phipps burned his lips on a tin cup of hot coffee. He laughed at the thought of the expression on Phipps face and what he said. "Goddamn cup done melted my lips," he had hollered,

185

much to the delight of the other troopers in the patrol.

Tye's thoughts ended suddenly when he was sure he heard something splash in the river. He was like a statue, all senses suddenly alert. He heard it again, closer. Staring into the darkness, he finally made out three riders...Apache riders. He shifted slightly to bring his rifle up when he heard a noise behind him. "What the hell?" he muttered under his breath. He turned to look behind him and was looking straight at another Apache that had come from he didn't know where. The Apache saw him when he turned but was a little slow in bringing up his rifle and Tye's bullet cart wheeled him backwards off the pony. Almost immediately bullets from the others were splattering rock fragments around him. He had no place to go but higher, up the cliff. When Tye reached the top his heart sank. From what he could see, he was in a lot of trouble. The top of the cliff angled sharply upwards about forty yards. It dropped forty feet straight down on two sides, a rock wall about fifteen feet high at the far end, and three Apaches coming up this end. The top was clean, no rocks, no pebbles and very little brush of any kind to hide behind.

He stood up and sprinted up the slope to the base of the rock wall at the far end. He found a boulder there large enough to protect him if he lay flat. "Thank you God." He lay flat and reloaded his rifle, laying his pistol at his side within easy reach and waited. Within a few seconds he saw the outline of a man coming over the rim and he fired his rifle at the shadowy figure. He knew he had missed but at least it bothered them enough to make them keep their heads down. 'This could get nasty,' he thought to himself as he reloaded the rifle. He glanced at the sky and saw heavy clouds moving in that would block any light from the moon which was coming up. "Give me a break,

Lord. Help me out some." The clouds were going to make it pitch black, and he knew what was going to happen. The Apaches would take advantage and sneak up under the darkness and his scalp would be hanging from one of their lances.

"Two can play that game," he said quietly. He took off his belt and made a sling for his rifle. He loosened his gun belt and sitting on his knees, slipped the holster around to where it was resting on his butt and slung the rifle over his shoulder. He was going to crawl down the slope as the Apaches were coming up the slope and he didn't want his pistol or holster scrapping the rock face of the slope and giving him away. He took his bowie out and held it in his right hand and had his pistol in his left. He checked the clouds again and then lay on his belly and started down, a few inches at a time. Every few seconds he would stop, straining hard to see thru the inky darkness, listen, then move again. This was repeated several times when he suddenly stopped. Had he heard something? He was laying perfectly still, holding his breath, every nerve on edge. He heard it again just to his right...sounded like a slight scraping sound. His eyes burned with the sweat running into them, even though it was very cool. He hadn't moved or hardly breathed for a full minute before he heard it again, above him. He was elated. He had passed one of them and the Apache had probably not been more than four or five feet from him. He lay there another minute or so and then started on down the slope, moving a little faster now as he felt he had passed thru them.

Just as he reached the bottom of the slope it was suddenly a little lighter and it startled him. The clouds had broke for just a few seconds and the slope, with its bleached white surface lit up. He turned and saw the Apaches about three fourths the way up the slope. He dropped off the end of the slope to where he had been earlier. He could hear the Apaches talking. "Probably wondering where that damn white man went," he muttered. He looked up at the clouds and knew it was fixing to get dark again as the opening in the clouds was closing fast. He wanted to get to the flat ground and be on the move away by then.

A couple steps from the bottom a rock gave way and he lost his balance and hit the ground hard. He was up quickly and heard the Apaches shouting and knew they were coming. Cussing his luck, he looked at the clouds again and figured there was only a few seconds of light left. He stopped, took his rifle off his shoulder, turned and aimed it at the rim. A second later one of the braves appeared on the edge. He started to yell and point at Tye but the words never came out as Tye's bullet smashed into his throat. He fell backwards on the slope, holding his throat, gurgling, drowning in his own blood. Grey Owl and the other brave rushed to his side just as his hands dropped to his sides, gasped a couple of times, and died.

Just as Tye figured, the clouds shut out all the light again and he could not see three feet. He knew the general direction the draw was in and headed that way, even though he could not see it. Moving quickly, he damn near fell in it when he got there, but he managed to keep his balance and found an easy way down. He stopped and listened but could hear no sound, which didn't surprise him. The Apache could move like ghost, even in darkness like this.

Moving down the draw rapidly, the only sound was the soft whisper of his moccasins on the damp, sandy bottom of the draw. He had gone what he thought to be far enough and climbed out of the draw.

He kneeled down on one knee and listened. He remembered he had not reloaded his rifle and started to do so, but stopped. No way could he do that without the metallic click of opening the chamber giving him away in the stillness of the night. He took out his pistol, and checked to make sure his Bowie was in his boot sheath. He got his bearings and figured Sandy was to his right, not far away. Moving in that direction he heard a sound and stopped. He heard it again and his brain was trying to decipher what it was. He took a couple more steps then he knew what it was; Sandy, munching on the short grass. Sandy nickered when he saw Tye. "No, don't do that, Sandy," Tye whispered as he put his hand on Sandy's nose. He held Sandy's mouth and nose to keep him quiet, and he listened for any other noises.

Hearing none, he mounted up. "Sandy," he whispered. "You can see in this darkness better than me. Get us out of here." He kicked him in the flank and Sandy damn near jumped out from under him. He hadn't gone twenty feet when both of the Apaches stood up in front of Sandy, and yelling, tried to make him buck and throw the white man off. They didn't know Sandy...their mistake. Sandy barreled into the one directly in front and knocked him ass over heels. The other jumped to the side and grabbed Tye by the arm and jerked him off Sandy.

Tye hit hard, losing his pistol in the fall. The Apache was on him quick and struck out at his head with his tomahawk. Tye, even though he was stunned was alert enough to thwart the blow with his arm, resulting in a nasty, painful cut on his upper arm. He struck up with his right and caught the Apache flush on the chin, rocking his head back and knocking him cold.

Tye jumped up to find the other Apache, but there was no need. Sandy had stomped his face to a pulp.   He hurried over to Sandy, opened his saddle bag and took out a piece of rawhide rope.   He flipped the unconscious Apache over on his stomach and grabbed his arms pulling them behind his back and tied them securely.   He got the extra canteen from the saddle, took a long drink and poured some in his hat and gave Sandy a drink.   He grabbed some jerky and sat down to relax for a moment. He rolled himself a smoke and noticed his hand was shaking slightly.   He figured it was due to the excitement and tension of the last two hours and a lot to the fact he was just plum exhausted.   All this, plus the fact his arm hurt like hell. He got another piece of rawhide and tied the brave's feet together then rechecked his hands.   Satisfied he took Sandy's saddle off, rubbed him down and gave him an extra long scratching between the ears.   "You saved my hide tonight old boy.   Thanks."   He grabbed Sandy around the neck and gave him a hug. "You're something special, feller."   He poured some water on his arm and cut up an old spare shirt he carried in his saddle bag and wrapped the wound as tight as possible.   He took the saddle blanket and bed roll and spread them out, lay down and was asleep immediately; knowing Sandy would wake him if there was danger.

Sandy, nickering and stomping his feet, woke Tye up three hours later... about two a.m...   The Apache was struggling, trying to free himself. The cloud cover was gone and things could be seen more clearly now.   Tye walked over to him.   "I'll be dammed if it ain't old Grey Owl himself."   Grey Owl recognized Tye and as their eyes locked on one another, Tye felt a shiver go up his spine.   Never had he seen such hate in a man's eyes.   They were on fire and burned right thru to Tye's inner soul.   Tye took the rope from around his feet and made a loop and put the loop around Grey Owl's neck. He saddled Sandy, mounted him and motioned for the Apache to start walking. Grey Owl stood fast, not moving. Tye took his foot out of the stirrup and kicked him hard to get him started. Grey Owl reluctantly headed out, walking with his head held high and his back straight...proud as he could be. Tye knew this was one Apache that would never give up.

Chapter XVI

It was almost dusk when Tye saw the rider in the distance. It was too far to tell if it was a white man or Indian. He was going to play it safe and get out of sight till he was sure who it was. Taking Sandy into the rocks along with Grey Owl, he waited and watched. The closer the rider got the more familiar he looked to Tye. He knew it wasn't an Apache, but the bandits were just about as bad...so he waited.

"I'll be damn," he said loudly as he recognized the rider. He stepped out into the open and yelled, "HEY AUGUST, YOU LOST?" Dan August damn near had a heart attack, then was laughing and racing to where Tye was, dismounting before his mount was completely stopped.

"Good to see ya, Tye. Was looking for ya. Ya okay?"

"I'm alive, anyway," Tye answered. "As far as being okay, that's debatable," he said laughing.

"Who's that?" Dan asked, noticing the Apache laying on the ground.

"Grey Owl," Tye answered.

Dan walked over and looked. "I be damned. Where's the others?"

"Dead"

"Dead?" Dan questioned.

"Yep, dead as can be. The only thing deader is my butt and I would appreciate it if you would get that damn patrol here where I can get rid of him," pointing to Grey Owl, "so I can get me some rest."

"Ya know, you don't look so good now that I take a good look...course ya never did." He laughed, jumped on his horse and was gone. Tye sat down beside Grey Owl and offered him a drink. The Apache spit on him and Tye unleashed a right that knocked the unsuspecting man cold. "Trying to be decent to his kind is a waste of time," Tye muttered. "He will hate us till he's dead." He rubbed his skinned knuckles with his left hand, lay back against a large rock, and relaxed.

Five minutes later he heard the patrol coming... hooves slamming the rocks, swords rattling, and saddles squeaking. Tye was reminded again why the cavalry never could surprise the Apache. Opening his heavy eyelids was an effort. He saw Dan and Lt. Garrison headed his way at a gallop. "Never will understand why a man runs his horse when it ain't necessary," Tye thought to himself.

With great effort, Tye stood up and waited.

"Congratulations, Tye. Dan filled me in on everything." He looked over to Grey Owl. "That's him, huh?

"That's Grey Owl, alright. You'd best tell your men right off, he ain't whipped yet and he'll gut one of them if he gets half a chance, so stay on their toes when guarding him. I've been around some bad'uns before but he's so full of hate he's about to burst."

"Looks like he's tied pretty good to me." Garrison commented.

"Just warn your men, okay, Lieutenant."

"Right, I'll take care of it." He turned and shouted, "Corporal Phipps, front and center."

"Yes Sir." Garrison repeated what Tye told him about Grey Owl.

"Everything clear, Phipps?"

"Yes Sir. Very clear, Sir."

"Then get your prisoner and take care of him."

"Yes Sir," Phipps saluted and then he and another man picked Grey Owl up and walked him away. Grey Owl turned his head and shouted at Tye.

"What did he say?" Garrison asked.

"Don't know all of it but he said something to the effect that it wasn't over between him and me." Garrison looked at the Apache, seeing the look on his face and the tone of his voice, and shuddered.

"Glad that's you and not me the red bastard is mad at."

As tired as Tye was, he had to laugh. "Won't make no difference, Lieutenant, you or me. He'll kill anyone if he gets a chance. Let's get mounted and head back. I got me a pretty lady waiting." Garrison had to admit that. Rebecca was one of the prettiest ladies he had ever seen... and she was as nice as she was pretty. He envied Tye for a lot of different things...him having Rebecca as his wife was at the top of the list.

When they arrived at the base camp, it was past midnight. Tye was the center of lots of congratulations, slaps on the back, and handshakes from the troopers, and Captain Delacruz was the first in line. Tye told him he appreciated the attention but he needed some sleep. He left everyone, crawled under his wool blanket, and was asleep in minutes. Schuler woke him up a few minutes later.

"Heard you had a couple cuts, Tye. Better let me see them."

"Can't it wait till I get some sleep?"

"Infection don't wait. With all the wounds you've had, you better than anyone should know that. Now let me take a look." The wounds were not

194

serious but would be sore as all get out for awhile. They were cleaned and dressed and Tye went to sleep.

Dan was filling Delacruz in on what Tye had told him had happened. Delacruz shook his head. 'Four to one odds and he killed them one at a time and captured their leader,' he thought to himself. He was an amazing man to say the least. He checked on the prisoner, made a round of the camp, checking sentries, then found his bedroll and went to sleep. His last thought was what Garrison told him Grey Owl had said and his description of the look of pure hate on the Apache's face. He shuddered and went to sleep.

The night, what was left of it, passed quickly and the men were up and eating their breakfast when the scream startled everyone. Tye, dropping his plate, knew immediately what happened and was cursing as he ran to where Grey Owl was, knowing what he would find. He was not surprised to find a bleeding private and Grey Owl standing behind him with a knife at the soldier's throat.

"Waa...kins." He hollered in broken English. When Tye and the rest stopped, he spoke loudly in guttural Apache. "Waa...kins... dachizha litsoz go'she'." He hesitated a couple seconds then shouted, "Waa...kins izdzan." He then spit in Tye's direction.

"What the hell is he hollering?" McClellan asked.

"Called me a dirty yellow dog and a woman," Tye said. "I was wondering when he would get around to it."

"What does he want?"

The scout waited a minute before answering, listenening to the continuing barrage of insults thrown at him by Grey Owl. "He knows a hangman's noose is

195

waiting for him at the fort. For an Apache, that is a disgraceful way to die. He wants me to fight him, one on one... Apache style."

"He must be crazy if he thinks you will accept his challenge." Garrison said.

"Amen," muttered Delacruz.

"You two have a lot to learn out here," Tye said. "Man ain't got much out here except his word... and his reputation. If I don't accept his challenge, he will tell every Apache that visits him in the guardhouse that I was afraid of him and the word will spread. I have a certain reputation to defend and he knows it."

"Doesn't he know your reputation with a knife?" questioned Garrison.

Sure he does, but let me ask you a question. If you know you are going to die, had you rather die quickly or sit in a cell for days sweating a hanging?" Delacruz and Garrison both nodded their heads they understood what he was saying.

"I understand, Tye, but you don't have to prove anything to us," Delacruz said.

"I know that," Tye said. "The reputation is with the Apaches. I'm not one to blow his own horn, both of you know that, but I have ears and I hear things. The Apache have a certain respect for me. You can call it fear or whatever you want, and that would be gone if I don't do this."

"Why don't we just shoot him and say he was trying to escape," Garrison said. Tye jerked his head around and started to verbally berate him but saw he was smiling and knew he wasn't serious. Tye turned back and in his best Apache, yelled at Grey Owl his acceptance of his challenge, resulting in an immediate reaction from the Apache. He threw the private to the ground and picked up some dirt and threw it on the injured man. The other troopers started to rush in but were stopped in their tracks by Tye's booming voice.

"EVERYONE BACK OFF AND RELAX!"Tye shouted. "Form a circle about thirty feet across around Grey Owl."

He took his buckskin shirt off, rolled his shoulders, flexing and loosening his muscles. He also did a few squats to loosen his leg muscles and his left arm was real sore...more so than he had thought. Taking his Bowie he walked up to Grey Owl and stuck the knife into the ground and backed off a couple of steps. Grey Owl did the same.

"Captain, in thirty seconds, yell, go... real loud."

He turned back to Grey Owl and told him in Apache they would start when the captain yelled. Grey Owl nodded his head and stared into the eyes of this man that struck fear in the hearts of all Apaches; this man who had killed Tanza and his friends; this man who had destroyed his dreams. He was ready, flexing and squeezing his hand so tight his knuckles were white. He knew this man's reputation with a knife and that he was probably going to die, but to die fighting, dying like an Apache warrior, was better than the disgrace of being hanged. Besides, it was a good day to die.

The troopers gathered in a circle with a lot of talk about what was happening. None of them had ever seen a knife fight, Apache style. Each of them was glad it was Tye and not them that was facing the Apache. All eyes were on the two warriors as they crouched facing each other, waiting. It became suddenly very quiet as each man held their breath, waiting for someone to die.

"GO!" Shouted Delacruz and each of the two fighters dove for their knife, each trying to get the advantage on the other.

"Get him Tye," cried some. "Kill the red

bastard," yelled others. Their cries fell on deaf ears as Tye was fully concentrating on trying to wrest his knife hand from Grey Owl's vice like grip, and at the same time keep Grey Owl from jerking his knife hand free from his grasp. Tye's left arm, the injured one was being sorely tested holding on to the Apache's knife hand. Neither was making any head way so Tye took the initiative by falling backwards onto his back, pulling the surprised Apache with him. As he fell, Tye brought up his right foot and stuck it in Grey Owl's belly and as he hit the ground, straightened out his leg, throwing Grey Owl high into the air and doing a somersault. To those watching, it looked like Grey Owl was flipping in slow motion. He hit the ground on his back with a solid thud and you could hear the air go out of his body. Tye was on him quicker than a rattlesnake could strike, his knife flashing as it caught the rays of the early morning sun and flashed downward. Tye was surprised to see Grey Owl roll to the side, resulting in his knife sticking harmlessly into the rocky ground where the warrior's chest had been an instant earlier. Tye barely missed receiving a nasty cut by a vicious retaliation swipe at his midsection by Grey Owl. Both men were on their feet in an instant, crouched and circling each other, both aware that instant death was waiting for the one that made the first mistake.

The only sound now was the two men's feet shuffling on the ground and their rapid breathing. The troops had become silent, enthralled by what they were witnessing. Both men were feinting as they circled, watching, and remembering how the other reacted to their feint. Grey Owl was no pilgrim when it came to fighting, even though he was young, and Tye knew that it was going to take all his skills to subdue him. 'A little luck would help, too,' he thought to himself.

Tye, crouched and carrying his knife low to the ground, cutting edge up as did Grey Owl, feinted a high blow and then, using a trick his pa had taught him, shifted the knife to his left hand and plunged it into a temporarily confused Grey Owl's upper thigh. Great amounts of blood spewed forth when he pulled his blade out. Grey Owl never missed a beat and striking down, almost caught Tye flat footed. Only Tye's quick reflexes saved him, but still received a nasty gash across his upper abdomen. A half an inch was the difference of having a shallow cut or being gutted like a deer. Both men were bleeding now but the leg wound of Grey Owl was pumping life giving blood out of him with every heart beat.

Realizing his strength was flowing out of him, Grey Owl rushed in to end it one way or the other. He came in bringing his knife from low to the ground toward Tye's midsection. Tye stepped aside and brought his razor sharp Bowie down on the Indian's wrist that held his knife. The wound and pain caused Grey Owl to drop his knife and Tye was on him, throwing him to the ground on his stomach and immediately was straddling the Apache's back, pinning him to the ground. Tye lifted Grey Owl's head up by pulling his hair, exposing his neck. Tye started the fatal plunge but reversed the knife and struck Grey Owl in the temple with the blunt end of the handle, knocking him out.

Standing up, chest heaving, Tye looked down at the warrior, then at Delacruz. "Get the surgeon here to fix him up. He's still going to hang." He walked over to a wagon where the water barrel was. The men parted, letting him thru. They were not whooping and hollering but were reserved, still in awe of what they had witnessed. One old trooper, an educated man, commented that he felt like one of the old Romans, watching the gladiators fight. The man next to him asked him who the hell the gladiators were. The old trooper had to laugh and tell him to never mind, it wasn't important.

Passing Tye, the surgeon stopped to look at Tye's cut that he was pouring water on to cleanse it. "Not serious, Tye, but it will be sore later. I'll patch you up in a minute... just as soon as I patch up the damn Apache. Seems a waste of time, since he's going to hang anyway."

"Just patch him up, Doc. He's caused a lot of misery out here and dying quick would be too easy on him. I want to see him hang." Delacruz and Garrison came over to Tye to check on him.

"You okay?" Delacruz asked.

"Just a scratch, Captain. Nothing to worry about." Delacruz looked at the six inch long gash and looked at Garrison...both shook their heads. They both knew he had come within a half a damn inch of being killed.

A half hour later, things had calmed down some but a few of the men were still talking about the fight. Most couldn't wait to get back and tell others about it. Doc had patched Grey Owl's leg and wrapped his head where Tye had busted it. Grey Owl was pretty damn upset with things. He was still alive, could not say Watkins had not fought him fair, his leg hurt something fierce, his head throbbed and he was headed for a hanging. It wasn't going to be a good day.

Doc had come back by and patched up Tye. "Another scar, boy. One or two more is all you have room for." He left shaking his head. Tye bent over to pick up his saddle and immediately knew that he was going to be in for a sore couple of days as his wound pained him something fierce. He carried the saddle over to Sandy and grimaced as he threw the blanket over Sandy's back. Corporal Phipps happened to see his expression and told Tye he would saddle Sandy. "Appreciate it Phipps. Damn stomach gonna be sore as hell for awhile."

"Least I could do for you after that entertainment you gave us."

"Well, it sure as hell wasn't by choice, Phipps."

"What do you mean?"

"Grey Owl is going to be in the guardhouse for awhile and he will have a visitor or two while he is there. Like I told Delacruz and Garrison earlier, the Apaches have a certain fear of me because I think like they do, fight like they do, and can track as well as them. If he told one other Apache that I refused his challenge, that fear, or maybe the respect they have for me, would be gone. My pa always told me to always do what you say you are going to do and never walk away from a fight when someone challenges you. Whether you win or lose doesn't matter, just don't walk away. I take that as meaning both white and red men."

"I understand, Tye. Hadn't thought of that. I'm sure you know that you don't have to prove anything to any of us." Phipps stared to say something else but stopped at Delacruz's order to mount up. "See you later, Tye." Tye nodded and mounted Sandy...gingerly, holding his hand on his stomach. The column moved out a minute later with Tye taking his position out front with Dan...heading home.

Chapter XVII

The dispatch rider Captain Delacruz had sent ahead arrived at Thurston's office about mid afternoon. Thurston opened it quickly; anxious to see what information it held.

Major Thurston
11/Oct/68
Post Commander
Fort Clark, Texas

Sir:
We had two engagements with the Apaches. All but four were killed. Grey Owl escaped along with three members of his band. Mr. Watkins tracked them down and killed all but one, Grey Owl. Watkins captured him and he is in custody.
Should be arriving shortly after dark. Several dead and several more wounded. Will need immediate medical attention.

Your Obedient Servant

Captain Horatio Delacruz.

Thurston was elated. Even his butt felt better with the news from Delacruz. He also knew he would have some information about that skunk Taggart as soon as Tye 'interviewed' the prisoners. He lit a cigar and sat back in his chair and for the first time in several days, relaxed. He called his orderly in and told him to find Raines, his interpreter. He sat back and enjoyed his cigar while waiting.

Word had spread like wildfire about the patrol's return tonight. Hearing of it, Sergeant O'Malley headed toward Rebecca's house to tell her the news but changed his mind and decided to let his wife tell her. Mrs. O'Malley hurried over to Rebecca's to give her the news. Rebecca was elated and couldn't hold back the tears. She told her friend that she had a lot of things to do... washing clothes and cleaning house. Mrs. O'Malley laughed and told her Tye only wanted to see her and could give a damn about anything else. "You just take you a hot bath and look pretty for him, honey. You're what he wants, not a clean house." She said laughing and hugging Rebecca again before she left.

Alone, Rebecca sat down in her favorite rocker and shut her eyes, thinking about Tye. It had been almost a week since he last held her and she needed him badly. She got up and put water on the stove to heat, got her tub out and filled it part way with water from the pump. She locked the door and undressed. She walked over to the mirror and looked at herself, checking to make sure she wasn't getting fat or sagging in the wrong places. Satisfied, she poured part of the hot water in the tub and settled in, laying her head back, relaxing, and thinking of the last time Tye made love to her. For Tye to be the big, fierce fighter he is, he was exceptionally tender in the way he touched her. She was ready for him to hold her tonight.

~~~

James Taggart was tired of being holed up in the small hotel room in Uvalde. He had been here it seemed forever, leaving only to go to the outhouse. His meals had been brought to his room by the giant, Edgar, his only friend and body guard. He had made himself scarce since he heard about his partner, Meechum's, arrest. As far as he knew, the only person that knew he was here was the hotel clerk and a few dollars under the table had shut his mouth. They had money stashed at the ranch and he intended to get it and then disappear. He would lay low forty-eight more hours then go to the ranch, get the money, get rid of Edgar and head to San Antonio. There was not near as much money as there would have been if it hadn't been for that damn nosey Watkins, but with Meechum in jail, there wasn't going to be a split, so he would come out okay. He lay down on the bed and smiled, thinking about the money and San Antonio.

~~~

About sundown, Rebecca joined other wives sitting by the bridge, waiting on their men to arrive, praying they are sitting in the saddle and not laid across it. They all heard about the casualties and there was very little talk among them and a lot of tension. Mr. and Mrs. O'Malley showed up a few minutes later, along with Thurston and several troopers. Thurston walked over to Rebecca.

"When they get here, I need Tye for a short time and then he's all yours, if that's okay. I know you are anxious to see him but I need to talk to him first."

"Of course it's okay. Just make it quick," she said, smiling.

"THEY'RE COMING!!" cried an excited voice

from one of the townspeople from across the bridge in Brackett. All the wives gathered at the bridge, nervously waiting, their eyes searching thru the fading light for a glimpse of their men.

Rebecca was running across the bridge when she saw Tye. Tye bent down and kissed her and then continued across the bridge, Rebecca reaching up and holding his hand, walked beside Sandy. Other wives did the same as each spotted their man. A lot of words and threats were coming from some of the townspeople when they spotted Grey Owl. Troopers moved up to form a barrier between them and the Apache.

"You okay, Tye?" Rebecca asked looking up.

"No serious damage, honey. Not enough anyway to hinder my plans for you." She smiled, squeezing his hand.

"I hope not," she said smiling.

Major Thurston came up to them and holding Sandy's bridle, told Tye he needed him for a few minutes. Tye dismounted, and put his arm around Rebecca, telling her he would see her at the house shortly.

"Have me a bath ready, okay?

"Figured I would," she said wrinkling her nose. Tye laughed, knowing he smelled to high heaven of horse, wood smoke, and sweat. One of the troopers took Sandy and Delacruz's horses to the stables. Tye and the captain followed Thurston to his office to give a verbal report. It took about twenty minutes for all the details to be described by Tye and Delacruz. When they were thru, Thurston told Tye he needed to see him first thing in the morning.

"Early?" Tye questioned.

Thurston smiled, "early as you can."

Tye left the Post Headquarters and headed

across the parade ground to his home about a hundred fifty yards away. Tye was anxious to get home to Rebecca but the walk took longer than it should have as he was stopped several times by soldiers congratulating him and asking questions. Tye, knowing how important his relationship was with the men patiently spoke with each one and answered their questions. When he finally arrived home and stepped on the porch, he saw a note pinned to the door.

'Don't even think about coming into this house wearing those smelly clothes.'

It was dark so Tye stripped off all his clothes, leaving them in a pile on the porch. He stepped into the house and saw Rebecca sitting on the edge of the tub, naked. In the low light of the lamp, she was an awesome sight. He stared for a moment, drinking in the sight of her beautiful body. She motioned for him to come to the tub with her finger. She watched him walk toward her admiring the hard muscled body of her husband...seeing his obvious excitement of the moment. When he got close she noticed the cut on his stomach.

"What is that?" she asked, dropping on her knees in front of him and touching the cut.

"Just a scratch. Nothing to worry about, honey." He pulled her to her feet and pulling her to him, embraced her, telling her how much he missed her and how much he loved her.

Her heart was pounding as she felt him pressing against her and it took all her will power to get him into the tub instead of the bed. Once he was in the warm tub, she walked to the stove to get the hot water. He lay back, closed his eyes, and relaxed for the first time in days and then was shocked when she poured the hot water in

"DAMN! You trying to get me clean or cook

me?" She laughed heartily at the joke and shoved Tye's head under the water. She then washed his hair, face, and neck, then his chest and back.

"Stand up," she ordered, and he did. She washed his stomach and on down his body. She handed him a towel and then ran and jumped into bed, waiting for what she knew was going to be a long, sleepless night, and it was.

Thurston was in his office when Tye arrived the next morning about-nine a.m...

"Glad to see you made it early," he said jokingly.

"Tough getting out of bed, Major. I was plum tuckered out."

"I can't imagine why," Thurston said smiling.

"What was so all fired important that I had to come over this morning?" Tye asked remembering the sight of Rebecca asleep when he left, the blanket only up to her waist as she lay on her back.

"Taggart!" Thurston said. "We can't find him or the big guy with him and Meechum won't talk and his men are so afraid of him, they won't either. I would like you to 'interview' them, alone of course, and see if you can get them to talk."

"When you say 'interview' do you mean in private, like I did with those Mexicans in getting the info about Alex and Frank Vasquez?"

"Exactly the same. I am bound by the military code of ethics or I would. You'll be alone." He handed Tye a piece of paper. "This will give the guard permission for you to enter the guardhouse with the key, alone. How or what you do to get the information is up to you. What I don't know, I can't do anything about."

"Won't take long, Major." Tye left and headed for the guardhouse across the parade ground. Thurston watched him leave from his office window and thought, "this damn army had more like him around the country, and there would be no Indian or bandit trouble to speak of."

Chapter XVIII

Tye gave the guard the note from Thurston. He looked at Tye, started to say something and decided not to. He unlocked the door to the guardhouse and gave the keys to Tye, shutting the door behind Tye when he entered. The strong smell of sweat mixed with excretion hit Tye's nose. He knew they had not taken out the waste buckets yet. When his eyes got accustomed to the dim light he walked to the cells. Three men were in the first two and one in the third.

"Howdy boys," Tye said jovially. The men did not move nor say anything. "Hope they are treating you okay."

"Who the hell is this character?" Came a voice from the back of the cell.

"Glad you asked, partner. My name is Tye Watkins and I'm in charge of your entertainment this morning." Heads snapped around, feet hit the floor, and someone said "shit." It was silent for a moment until Tye asked.

"Which one of you gentlemen is the toughest, meanest sonofabitch of the lot?" No one said a word. Tye pulled his gun and waved it at the men in the first cell. "Back against the wall, all of you...except you." He pointed to a very large, tough looking man that had a long scar across his right cheek.

"You step outside of the cell."

"Maybe I don't want" ...he didn't finish as Tye quickly switched his gun to his left hand and unleashed a right to the midsection that doubled the surprised man over. Tye grabbed his hair and flung him outside of the cell, stepped out, shutting the door and locking it behind him.

The man got his wind back and straightened up. "Where can I find Taggart?" Tye asked.

"Who's Taggart?" the big man answered back.

"Wrong answer," Tye hollered as he struck him in the stomach again. As the man folded over, Tye's knee came up hard, catching him full in the face, smashing his nose and knocking out a couple of teeth. The man was holding his hands to his face, blood running between his fingers when Tye hit him again in the stomach. The big man doubled over and hit the floor groaning. Tye walked to the cell door, opened it and dragged the man inside.

He looked at the men in the cell who had moved against the far wall. "Where is Taggart?" Silence greeted his answer. "This is going to be a fun day...for me," he said. He pointed to a young, well built man.

"You're next," and motioned him to come outside the cell. "And don't get me riled by having to come get you." The young man hurried out of the cell, and cowered against the far wall, wondering what was in store for him. He found out immediately as Tye pitched him his bowie knife. "Know how to use that?" Tye asked. "You can be a hero to the rest of the scum in this place, if you can kill me." The young man dropped his hand holding the knife to his side. "You had better use it son, or I'm gonna stick it up your butt."

211

The other men shouted encouragement to the young man and he dropped into a crouch, holding the knife in front of him. Tye knew this was going to end quickly as the man knew nothing about handling a knife, a gun maybe, but not a knife. The man lunged, swinging wildly like Tye figured he would. Tye stepped back, let the man's momentum carry him by and then grabbed him from behind, holding the man's knife hand and pulled hard, spinning the man around. He held the man's arm straight with his right hand and brought his left down hard across the forearm. The bone snapping could be heard by everyone before the man screamed in pain.

Once again, Tye opened the door and dragged the injured man in. "Anyone want to tell me where Taggart is now, or do we continue having fun? Three or four men spoke at once. "What exactly do you want to know?" They were scared of this crazy man and wanted no part of him. "Only one thing... where can I find Taggart?" He got his information and was sure it was good information. If it wasn't, he promised a return visit and he wouldn't be so nice.

~~~

Thurston wasn't surprised when Tye returned and told him to send the surgeon to the guardhouse. He was elated when Tye told him where not only to find Taggart but where the money was hidden at the ranch.

"CORPORAL JAMESON!" Thurston shouted at this orderly. A chair could be heard scraping the floor and then falling over as the orderly hurried to the door. Tye smiled and thought to himself, "damn troopers are trained to jump like a scared rabbit when he hollers."

"Yes Sir, Major," the orderly said saluting.

"Get me Captain Delacruz and Lieutenant

212

Garrison immediately."

Thurston and Tye walked over to the wall map. Thurston placed his finger on a spot northwest of Uvalde.

"Meechum's ranch is about here," he said.

Tye studied the map for a moment. "Must be close to the Mendoza's ranch."

"You're familiar with the area then?" Thurston questioned, though not surprised. Seems Tye knew about every settler for fifty miles in every direction of Clark.

"Been a long time since I visited them, but yeah, I know the area."

Thurston walked to his stuffed chair and sat down, took out a cigar and offered Tye one. "Thanks, Major." Thurston lit his and then Tye's, both inhaling the tobacco deep, enjoying the flavor.

"Nothing to relax a man like a good cigar," Thurston said leaning back in the chair.

"Only other thing would be a good shot of strong whiskey to go with it," Tye countered.

"Or maybe some good loving from a beautiful woman," Thurston said smiling, obviously referring to Rebecca. Tye just smiled, making no comment.

"What's the plan, Major?

"I intend to ..."a knock on the door interrupted his answer.

"COME."

The orderly stepped in. "Captain Delacruz and Lieutenant Garrison are here, Sir."

"Good. Send them in." Delacruz and Garrison stepped in, stopped and saluted.
Returning the salute, Thurston instructed them to come in and sit down.
"Tye, here," he paused trying to come up with a good word but could not, "interviewed the prisoners and got

213

some information about the whereabouts of Taggart and also the possible location of the money they got for the stolen cattle. I know you just got back from a long patrol but I thought, since both of you are involved deeply in this, you might want to be on hand when it's finished."

Both men answered at the same time. "Yes Sir."

"Good," Thurston said, walking to the wall map. "This is where Meechum's ranch is." He placed his finger on the map marking the spot. "Captain, I want you to get O'Malley and take a detail to the ranch. O'Malley was there the other day and can show you the way. The money is supposedly under the floor under the table in the kitchen. There is a rug over it. Lieutenant, I want you to accompany Tye to Uvalde. Our information says he has a friend that runs a hotel there. We're hoping he is holed up there. Take four men with you. Any Questions?"

"When do we leave, Sir?" Delacruz asked.

"Right away; just as soon as we can get a few supplies together. Maybe in a hour."

"We'll meet at the stable in an hour then," Tye said.

"Good luck men," Thurston said, shaking each of their hands as they left.

Tye headed back home, dreading having to tell Rebecca of his leaving again so soon. When he arrived, Rebecca was walking out of the house.

"Where are you going?" Tye asked.

"Over to O'Malley's. I thought you might be there."

"I've been at Thurston's office. Let's sit on the porch and talk."

Rebecca hesitated for a minute, telling by Tye's tone that it was news she didn't want to hear. She took his hand and walked with him to the porch, bracing herself for the news.

"I got some information from the prisoners today about where Taggart may be. He's caused a lot of deaths out here honey, and he needs to be brought in to pay for them. The Indian trouble will not end until he is behind bars. I'm to go to Uvalde with Garrison to get him and bring him back. After that, I'm yours for awhile, at least till you get tired of me being under your feet."

Rebecca put her head on his shoulder to keep him from seeing her tears. "How long?"

"May be back tomorrow night... day after at the latest."

"When are you leaving?

"About an hour."

"Then we better hurry?"

"Hurry? Hurry for what?" Tye asked.

"This," she stepped back and started unbuttoning her dress. Tye smiled, took her by the arm and entered the house, locking the door...

The patrol, consisting of Tye, Delacruz, Garrison, O'Malley, and six troopers, were on the Old Mail road headed to Uvalde. They would stay together for several miles before Delacruz headed northeast toward the ranch. About two p.m., they passed the place where Tye found the missing payroll wagon and the murdered escort back in July. The old wagon was still on its side, just off the road. Tye noticed how green everything was. "Had a lot of rain along here," he thought to himself. The purple sage was in bloom and it's light gray, or blue was in stark contrast with the green of the grass, mesquite, and cedar. About ten miles from Uvalde, they took a break.

"We need to head northeast after the break, Sir," O'Malley said to Delacruz.

Delacruz nodded. "Figured it was getting about time."

"How much further to Uvalde, Tye?" Garrison asked.

"Ten or so miles; we'll be there about sundown." Fifteen minutes later, their break over, they mounted up and split, each group headed to their assigned destination.

Chapter XIX

The room was almost dark when Taggart woke up from his nap. He stood up, smoothed out his clothes, walked to the window, and pulled the curtain back to look out on the street below. He was surprised at how few people were milling about. He was in a good mood for the first time in days. He decided to hell with waiting to get the money, he was going out to eat, have a few drinks and then go to the ranch at first light. There was a knock on the door and he knew it was Edgar, coming to get what he wanted brought to his room to eat.

"Whatcha wanna eat, boss?"

"Let's go downstairs to the restaurant and then go have a drink."

Edgar had a surprised look on his face. "Ya sure that's a good idee?"

"I'm tired of being cooped up in this stinking room. I need to get out to stretch my legs and get some damn fresh air." He put on his black coat, retied his string tie, and walked to the door. "Let's go."

His friend, the hotel clerk, did a double take when he saw Taggart coming down the stairs. He hurried over to him. "There's soldiers in the restaurant," he warned.

"Inge or Clark soldiers?"

"Why, they're Inge, but what does that have to do with anything?"

"Never mind." He fumbled in his pocket and brought out some bills and handed them to Edgar. "Go to the saloon next door and wait on me there." Edgar took the money and turned to leave when Taggart added, "and don't get drunk." Edgar only nodded. Taggart figured if the Inge soldiers were looking for him, they would know him if he came in with Edgar. Edgar was hard to miss because there wasn't that many men his size. He went into the restaurant and sat down to enjoy his meal.

It was full dark when Tye and the detail rode into town. Tye was surprised the town had grown as much as it had since he was here. Instead of one hotel and one saloon that he remembered, he could see two hotels and at least three saloons. They stopped in front of the first saloon they came to. Tye and Garrison dismounted, handing their reins to one of the soldiers. Tye looked over the batwing doors into the interior of the saloon. Most of the tables were empty and the patrons were a mixed lot; none of whom Tye recognized. They walked a few doors down to another saloon that had someone playing a piano and the sound of a woman's voice trying to carry a tune. The rest of the soldiers, still mounted, walked their horses in the street, staying abreast with Tye and Garrison. Tye looked thru the dirty window and immediately saw the big man who was with Taggart.

"There's the big sonofabitch that is with Taggart," he said to Garrison. "I don't see Taggart anywhere though." He did notice that the men in the saloon were a rough looking lot. They sure as hell didn't look like working citizens of Uvalde.

"How we going to handle this?" Garrison asked.

"I'm thinking on it," Tye replied. He didn't really want to bust in on the big guy not knowing where the main man was. He didn't give a damn about the big guy. He sure as hell didn't want to spook Taggart if he was close by and then have to find him again. Looking around he saw a livery stable across and just down the street.

. "Let's put the horses in that livery stable," he said pointing across the street. "Maybe the liveryman will let us stay there for awhile if we tell him what we are doing and who we are looking for."

The liveryman liked to talk and he was filling Tye in on Taggart. "Came in with the biggest sonofabitch I ever did see...ugliest, too." Tye had to laugh along with Garrison.

The man continued. "Didn't like him right off. One of those that think they are better than the rest of us folks. Treated the big man like he was a damn dog. You know, telling him to go there, do this, sit, talk, and all that shit. Just don't like the bastard." He paused for a minute then asked, "whatcha looking for him for?"

"Caused a lot of problems with the Apaches that led to a lot of innocent people being killed, both white and Apache," Tye answered.

"Lieutenant," One of the soldiers whispered. Both Tye and Garrison turned toward the man. "I think that's Taggart going into the bar that you just looked in thru the window."

Tye and Garrison only got a glimpse of him. "You sure?" Garrison asked looking at the trooper.

"Pretty sure. I saw him a couple of times before," the soldier said.

"I'll take a look-see." Tye said and started across the street. He peered thru the same window he looked thru earlier and saw Taggart just sitting down with the big man.   Tye hurried back to the livery stable. "Good job, trooper," he said shaking the private's hand. "He's there, Lieutenant."

"Let's get this over with then," Garrison said. "Let's go," and started out of the livery stable.

"Hold on, Lieutenant," Tye said placing his hand on the Lieutenants shoulder.   "There is a rough looking crowd in there. I'd be willing to bet Taggart ain't the only one that the army or the law is looking for. If we go busting in there, things could get a little out of hand with them not knowing its not them we're looking for."

"What do you suggest then?"

"Me and you go in and walk up to the bar and order a drink and see what happens."

"What about the rest of my men?"

"Put two in the back of the saloon to watch the back door and have the other two wait at the door to help if we need it."   They started across the street with two of the soldiers hurrying between the buildings to get in back of the saloon.

~~~

Delacruz and his detail arrived at the ranch just after dark.   Entering the main house, he stumbled around some in the darkness before he found and lit the kerosene lamp. O'Malley moved the table and pulled back the rug under it.   Sure enough, just as the prisoners said, they saw a trapdoor in the floor.

"Open it up, O'Malley," he ordered.   "Let's see what's there."   O'Malley fumbled with the latch for a moment, trying to get his fingers under the latch.

"Damn latch must have been made for a kid's hand," he mumbled before he finally got it open. Reaching down in the dark hole he fumbled around for

221

a couple seconds.

"Got it, Captain," he said bringing out a heavy looking sack. He stood up and placed it on the table. Delacruz untied the rawhide strings that bound it and emptied the contents on the table. A lot of silver and gold coins were rolling around on the table. Large wads of paper money fell out, also.

O'Malley let out a low whistle. "That's the most damn money I ever saw in my life."

"We need to count it, Sergeant." Delacruz took a chair, as did O'Malley, and they started to total it up. When they finished, it was almost twenty five hundred dollars. Delacruz made a tally sheet and both he and O'Malley signed it and he put it in his pocket. They put the money back in the bag. "Let's get to Uvalde and see if Tye and Garrison are having any luck.

~~~

Tye and Garrison entered the saloon and as planned, neither looked in the direction of Taggart. At the bar, he glanced in the mirror and saw Taggart talking to the big man and both looking at them. Tye quickly turned his eyes away and ordered Garrison and himself a drink. He was fixing to take his first drink when he heard his name shouted.

"TYE WATKINS!!" Immediately, silence fell over the saloon. Even the piano player stopped playing. A low murmur went around the room that the man at the bar was the scout from Clark that everyone this side of San Antonio has heard about. Tye turned around, his back on the bar, elbows resting on the bar. The big man was coming towards him and he was fuming.

"WATKINS, I'M GONNA TEAR YOU APART." When he got closer, he mumbled something about Tye sucker punching him a few days earlier. Tye didn't move, but his muscles were tensed and ready. To all watching, he looked as calm as a man sitting in Church.

A stride from Tye, the big man swung his huge fist at Tye's head. Tye ducked and stepped aside. Edgar turned and swung again, and again Tye ducked, and moved. Garrison, who had been concerned at first with this giant, now relaxed. He had seen Tye like this before in a fight... he was playing with the big man. The man was huge, strong as a bear but even Garrison could see he was slow. Frustrated, Edgar swung again with a fist that could damn near knock a man's head off. Tye stepped back this time and then stepped in swinging a right fist that was placed just above the belt buckle of Edgar, knocking the air out of him. Tye stepped back, let him get his wind, and waited. When Edgar stepped toward him, Tye attacked surprising the man. A quick right caught the man on the cheek and a quick left followed that caught Edgar flat on the nose, breaking it again. Tye followed with two more blows to the midsection and a tremendous right upper cut that rocked Edgars head back and stood him straight up. He looked at Tye, blood running from his busted nose and a cut on his cheek, and slowly crumbled to the floor.

Tye turned his attention to Taggart but before he moved toward him, he spoke. "My name is Tye Watkins, Chief of Scouts out of Fort Clark. This man here is Lieutenant Garrison, and we have men in front and back of the saloon. I don't won't any trouble with any of you; we're here after this man," he said pointing to Taggart.

"Someone in the back of the room yelled. "Hell, take him Tye; we don't want no trouble with you or the army."

"Amen to that," said another as the men were astonished at how easy the big man had been taken down by Tye.

"You coming easy, or hard, Taggart?"

"I'm coming, dammit," Taggart said disgusted. "I'm coming." Taggart got up from his chair and walked toward Tye, cussing himself for deciding to come out in the open. He was so close... so damn close to getting the money.

"Let's go, Taggart. Your friends are waiting for you in the guardhouse at Clark. He took a step toward Taggart when Taggart pulled a hidden gun and shot at Tye. The bullet struck his left shoulder, spinning him around. Years of honing his survival skills and reflexes took over, and while being spun around by the force of the bullet, he reached down and pulled his Bowie and in one motion threw it at Taggart as the little man was fixing to shoot again. The ten inch Bowie buried itself to the hilt in Taggart's chest before anyone could even move. The little man was dead before he hit the floor. There was complete silence in the room, everyone stunned by the sudden turn of events including Garrison.

"TYE," he shouted, recovering from the shock." You hit hard?"

"Left shoulder," Tye uttered bending over holding his shoulder...blood running threw his fingers, down his arm and onto the floor.

Garrison bellowed. "One of you get the doctor, NOW." Two or three men ran into each other getting out of the saloon to find the doctor. Tye straightened up and walked over to the bar, picked up his drink and downed it in one gulp.

"Give me another," he said to the bartender. "And keep them coming till the doc gets here." His shoulder was hurting him something fierce but one would never know it by looking at him.

"Barkeep," one of the men in the saloon said loudly. "Don't even think about charging that man one cent for them there drinks... they're on me. Least I can do to pay for that show."

The doctor arrived before Tye finished his third drink. "Let's get that shirt off and take a look," he said. Garrison knew what was coming from the onlookers. He had seen Tye's muscular body and his scars before but each time someone new saw it, there was always a lot of comments. He wasn't disappointed.

"My God, man!" The doc exclaimed. "You have more damn scars than all the soldiers at Inge put together." He shook his head and looked at the wound. "Don't look like it hit bone. Went thru clean." He bandaged it up and put his arm in a sling. "You don't need to use that arm any more than you have to... and get some rest."

Garrison laughed out loud.

Doc looked at him. "What's so funny, Lieutenant?"

"You telling him to get some rest," he laughed and said, "If you ever saw his wife, you would know he would have to be dead to rest."

"Real funny, Garrison. Excuse me if I don't laugh," Tye said with a slight smile.

"Here's your knife, Mr. Watkins," a young man said. "I cleaned it for you, too."

"Thanks," Tye said, and with his good arm, reached out and shook the man's hand.

Edgar had been forgotten about during the excitement. When he came to and got his senses back, he had seen Taggart dead, with Tye's knife in his chest. He gathered himself and got up and walked over to Tye, bloody nose and all and stuck out his hand. He held Tye's hand for a moment and turned to the crowd. "Been whipping men all my life...never been beat. This here man done it twice." He looked at Tye. "You won't get a chance for a third," bringing a round of raucous laughter from everyone. He released Tye's hand and strolled over to the bar.

"What about him?" Garrison asked.

"What about him?" Tye replied. "He's just a big oaf that picked the wrong man to be his boss. Let him be."

"Delacruz is here," one of the troopers standing by the door shouted.

"Bring him in here, trooper," Garrison ordered. When Delacruz came in, Garrison filled him in on everything as did Delacruz to him.

"Guess it's time to head back," Delacruz said. "Tye, can you ride?"

Tye, thinking of a beautiful woman at the fort that would feel awful sorry for him and make sure he got taken care of proper, smiled in spite of the pain in his shoulder."Let's go, Captain."

~~~

Shakespeare had spent a day resting and making new friends at Fort Davis, including the Post Commander who invited him to be their Chief of Scouts right before he left. Shakespeare had told him thanks but he had to see Tye. He might come back and take him up on it, though.

Eight days later, he was enterering Brackett where he headed straight to the nearest saloon. He wasn't so much needing a drink as he was for finding out where Tye was. Where better to get information than from a barkeeper. So happens this saloon was Jim's, Tye's friend. Shakespeare entered thru the bat wing doors and got an immediate warm welcome from the friendly owner behind the bar.

"Come on in, stranger," the man said loudly, causing several of the patrons to turn and take a quick look at Shakespeare before going back to their drinking and visiting. "Jim's the name, friend," the bartender said reaching out to shake Shakespeare's hand. "Yours?" He asked.

"McDovitt...Shakespeare   McDovitt," Shakespear replied. "My frens kall me 'Buff'." There was a strange look on Jim's face as he held on to Shakespear's hand.

"The mountain man McDovitt?" Jim asked.

Shakespeare, surprised at him knowing his name replied. "Wus wun...long time ago. Why...how do yu kno my name?"

"If you're who I think you are you are, going to make a friend of mine the happiest man on this here earth."

"Whu mite this fren be?" Shakespeare asked.

"Tye...Tye Watkins," Jim replied and finally let go of Shakespeare's hand.

"Tye's whu I kame all this way ta see. Trapp'd fur yeers with his pa, Ben."

Jim whistled loudly and things got quite with every head turned his way. "Got an announcement, men; we have a man here you all need to meet." He turned to Shakespeare and placed his hand on Shakespeare's shoulder. "This here is the man some of you have read about in those novels about the mountain men and all of you have heard Tye talk about him at one time or another. Folks, this here is Shakespeare McDovitt, Tye's pa's best friend when trapping in those mountains."

Shakespeare was damn near crushed by the men wanting to shake his hand and pat him on the back.

"DRINKS ARE ON THE HOUSE," Jim shouted, his announcement followed by loud whooping and even a couple pistols being fired by the men.

Two hours later, a slightly drunk Shakespeare was being led by Jim across the bridge over Los Moras Creek and into Fort Clark. Jim had explained to Shakespeare that Tye was on patrol but should be back in the morning, and in the mean time he figured Shakespeare could stretch out in Tye's old quarters...if Major Thurston would allow him. They were headed to Thurston's quarters to find out. Jim figured there would be no problem, seeing how that this was Shakespeare and Thurston had heard about him for the last two years from Tye. He couldn't wait to see Tye's face when he met the man who had taught Ben everything that Ben had taught him.

"Yes sir. Tomorrow is going to be a great day," Jim muttered to himself.

Chapter XX

It had been a restless night for Shakespeare, one without a lot of sleep even though he had been a little drunk before going to bed. The excitement of what was going to happen had him on edge. He didn't remember ever being this nervous. It was still a couple hours before daylight as he got out of bed.

"To hell with trying to sleep," he muttered, and put his pants on. Barefoot, he stumbled around till he found the lamp on the table in the kitchen. After lighting the lamp, he opened doors till he found what he was looking for, coffee and a cup. Lighting the fire in the cook stove, he placed the water on to boil and walked back to the bedroom to finish dressing. The aroma of the coffee filled the room as soon as he dropped the grains into the boiling water. Filling his cup and sitting down, Shakespeare contemplated meeting his lifelong friend's son. He had just put the cup to his lips when a knock came on the door. Opening the door, he was looking at a young corporal.

"Major Thurston wants you to come to the hospital."

"Huspetal? Why tha huspetal?"

"Tye's there and he's been wounded. Major figured you would want to be there."

"Leed tha way, sunny."

When they arrived the first thing Shakespeare saw was the 'purtiest' woman he ever did see. She was standing beside Thurston. Thurston immediately

230

came over with the lady to Shakespeare.

"Shakespeare, this is Tye's wife, Rebecca. Rebecca, this is Shakespeare McDovitt."

"My pleazur, mam," Shakespeare said shaking her hand.

"Shakespear McDovitt!! The mountain man and Ben's friend?" Rebecca questioned.

"I wus Ben's frend bac in thos days."

"Oh my God," she said, tears flowing down her cheeks. Thurston handed her a handkerchief and after wiping her eyes, hugged the little man and kissed him on the cheek. "You are going to make my husband the happiest man on this earth." She hugged him again just as Tye, shirtless, and his arm in a sling, walked into the room. She ran to him and carefully hugged him, kissing him on the lips. "Are you okay?"

"Nothing a little tender loving care won't fix," Tye replied, smiling. He shook the major's hand.

"Another outstanding job, Tye. I would have rather had that skunk, Taggart alive to hang, but what the hell, he's dead and things ought to get better. He looked at Shakespeare who was standing off to one side thinking he was looking at a ghost. Tye was the spitting image of Ben, tall, muscular, blue eyes, and good looking.

"Tye, this is Shakespeare McDovitt," Thurston said. Tye shook Shakespeare's hand.

"Glad to meet you old timer," he said, surprised at the strong grip the little man had. He turned to leave with Rebecca. He took two steps, stopped and looked back at the little man. "What did you say your name was?"

"It's Shakespeare, honey. Your dad's friend from long ago," Rebecca whispered. Tye stared at the little man. "That true?"

"I wus Ben's frend bac in those days in tha Rockies."

"My God," Tye said as he walked up to Shakespeare.

"Ya luk jus' like Ben, Tye. When I saw ya a minete ago I tho't I wus luking at a ghost."

Tye looked at Rebecca and Thurston and both nodded their heads. He put his hand on Shakespeare's shoulder and pulled him against his chest. "Shakespeare. My God, Shakespeare," he said hugging the little man as tears welled up in his eyes. Shakespeare, surprised by the hug at first, wrapped his arms around Tye, tears welling up in his eyes also. Rebecca was crying and Thurston had to excuse himself from the emotional scene.

"Ya'll have a lot to talk about so I'll see you later, Tye."

Tye, with his good arm around Rebecca and in control of his emotions again, suggested they go to their house for something to drink.

"Shakespeare, you don't know how much I have wished for something like this; someone to talk to about how it was in those days; someone that might have known pa. I never thought it would happen though because it's been so long, and now...you're here. My God, do I have questions for you."

"I got plentee ta tale ya, Tye. Storee's tha Ben mite hav' told ya, but Ben weren't wun to brag on himself so I'm figguring he didn't tale ya all tha thangs he did. He wus a man's man, Tye, and I wus proud ta call him my fren."

"My pa's best friend...here...unbelievable. Let's go home. I want, more than anything, to hear those stories."